LOST IN SPACE

LOST IN SPACE

Novelization by

JOAN D. VINGE

Based on the screenplay by

AKIVA GOLDSMAN

HarperPrism
A Division of HarperCollinsPublishers

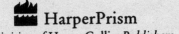 **HarperPrism**

A Division of HarperCollins*Publishers*
10 East 53rd Street, New York, N.Y. 10022-5299

This is a work of fiction. The characters, incidents, and
dialogues are products of the author's imagination and are not to
be construed as real. Any resemblance to actual events or
persons, living or dead, is entirely coincidental.

A hardcover edition of this book was published
in 1998 by HarperPrism.

ISBN 0-06-105908-0

HarperCollins®, ®, and HarperPrism®
are trademarks of HarperCollins*Publishers* Inc.

Cover illustration courtesy of New Line Cinema

First paperback printing: May 1998

Printed in the United States of America

Visit HarperPrism on the World Wide Web at
http://www.harperprism.com

❖ 10 9 8 7 6 5 4 3 2

To
*Lister and Mary
and the
Clarion Class
of '97*

*I wouldn't say it
if I didn't love it*

ACKNOWLEDGMENTS

The author is extremely grateful to
Melanie Orpen, for her help in
unravelling the Gordian Knot;
and also to Rich Miller and Jim Frenkel,
for getting the elephants over the Alps.

LOST IN SPACE

Prologue

"Hypergate Docking, this is *Grissom One*. Request final descent vector." The pilot of the *Grissom One* looked out at the view slowly filling the bubble dome of the ship's bridge, and smiled. There was no other choice, when you first saw this view. No matter how many times you saw it, it was like nothing else: the Earth hanging in space, a blue opal on black velvet ... and in the nearer distance the spires of the space station sitting like a crown on the surreal, ten-mile-circumference construct of the hypergate.

Construction workers looked up, their helmet faceplates mirroring sunlight as bright as their laser torches, to watch the ship's silhouette pass overhead. The gate's structure was almost finished; soon it would be humanity's first conduit through hyperspace.

"Roger, *Grissom One*, this is Hypergate Docking Control." Bill Randall's familiar voice was comfortably serene in her headset speakers. "You are cleared to land. Hope you got some Partagas in that rust bucket, Sal."

Sal grinned as she fed landing coordinates to the onboard computers and felt the ship's thrusters fire in response. The cargo vessel's trajectory began to shift slowly and precisely, aligning its angle of approach to the designated docking platform. "I brought you the most amazing—"

Randall never found out what. Death fell out of the starry night and exploded the *Grissom One*'s bridge, swallowing the freighter in a ball of fire.

Major Don West shifted in his gyroscopic harness, working the heads-up holographic display as his V-winged craft launched from the ASOMAC fighter base. The ship cut through the night like a silent scream as he vectored toward the expanding cloud of debris. The cockpit was a bubble of transparent alloy, set like a pearl at the nose of his craft; his controls gave him almost a 360 view of the hypergate ring, the freighter's remains at its center . . . and the enemy.

The gaping work crews vanished behind him in a heartbeat, while ahead of him the expanding blizzard of jagged shrapnel hurtled toward his ship . . . and toward the surface of the half-finished hypergate structure. Two blunt-nosed Sedition ships burst through the tumbling debris—the same ships that had just blown the freighter to bits.

"Who hit us?" Jeb Walker's voice demanded over his comm link.

The *Ranger One* entered West's peripheral vision, its extended wings taloned with gleaming weaponry; the twin of his own *Eagle One* except for its markings. He smiled as he saw the shark-toothed grin painted on Walker's right wing, and the cosmic Hand of Fate on the left.

His own wing bore an eagle's shadow and an eagle's eye; everything a hunter needed, nothing more. *Sometimes Jeb thought too much. . . .* But there was nobody he trusted more. Jeb had been his buddy, back watcher, and cheerful rival ever since their Academy days.

"Sedition raiders," West said grimly. "They've never come this far out before."

Walker grunted. "This cold war just got hot."

The enemy ships vectored across the hypergate's arc; their plasma cannons blasted gaping holes in its superstructure. West spun his controls, seeing the entire scene in one giddy rush as he veered off after the closest raider. "Last one to kill a bad guy buys the beer." He activated his targeting computer.

Whatever else the Sedition raiders were, they were good pilots. The insectoid ship, its angular arms bristling with weaponry, danced infuriatingly in and out of the crosshairs inside his holographic array. West fired, cursing in frustration as the attacker jagged upward at a ninety-degree angle, and his laser burst burned vacuum.

He dodged hurtling debris, closing in on the fleeing raider as if he and his ship shared a single mind. The fraction of his attention that was always watching his partner's back told him Walker had engaged the other attacker; the lancing bolts of energy were a psychedelic light show below his feet. "Hey Jeb," he called, glancing down, "I can see your house from here—"

The split second of distraction almost cost him, as the raider up ahead made a sudden coin-flip and hit its thrusters, firing nonstop as it came back at him.

A *game of chicken*. West grinned without feeling it as the enemy ship burned toward him. *He'd never lost one yet*. He returned fire, pushing his ship's speed, holding the collision course as the distance between his ship and the enemy fighter closed precipitously. "The band is warming up...." he murmured, and music was the furthest thing from his mind.

He didn't check his displays, didn't need to now; his gaze was locked on the closing ship. "The crowd begins to roar...." His grin widened. His eyes were filled with the dazzle of pulse lightning. He felt more alive now, on the brink of death, than he ever felt any other time.

A nova in the neon starfield of his displays was warning him of imminent collision as the attack ship's image flashed on his screen, captured in the targeting hash marks. The display expanded around him, becoming a tactical grid.

"Target lock," the computer said.

"The lights are dimming ..." He laughed, his voice rising with elation. "The curtain's coming up. Showtime!" He fired.

The laser bursts converged on the attacking ship, barely meters ahead of him. It exploded just off his bow. West screamed in exhilaration and giddy terror as his ship tore through a swarm of debris.

A spacesuited body slammed into the transparent wall in front of him. West jerked back; sucked in a deep breath, face-to-face with the anonymous corpse that would have been his own if his luck hadn't held. "While you're at it," he muttered, "check the oil."

In another moment the body was gone, and only the

gleaming curve of the hypergate lay ahead, cradling a lagoon of stars.

The second attack ship roared past below his feet, weapons firing, locked in a pinwheeling battle with Jeb's fighter. He watched Walker jag sharply, clearing the lethal fireworks of a high energy volley—almost.

A lash of energy grazed Jeb's ship; West grimaced as he saw the glowing furrow it plowed in the fusilage. Jeb's attacker looped the loop and was back on his tail already, firing.

"Weapons are off line." Walker's voice came through the headset phones, sounding as matter-of-fact as if he'd lost a pair of socks. "I'm gonna jettison the main drive core."

The thruster core of Walker's ship blew free in a bolus of flame, and West watched it fly back with the uncanny accuracy of an avenging sword blow to collide with the pursuing craft. He hooted with glee as the raider ship exploded in a ball of light.

"Am I good, or *what?*" Jeb crowed triumphantly.

West opened his mouth to reply, broke off as he heard Walker's sudden curse, half drowned in a burst of static. "Jeb . . . ?" he said.

The echo of a computer's synthesized voice answered him through Walker's open mike: "*Warning. Failure in redundant drive systems.*"

West swore as he looked up and realized where they were heading: *on a collision course with the hypergate.*

Static stung his ears, and an alarm began to sound aboard Walker's ship. "*Impact in ninety seconds,*" the onboard computer said.

"*Damn*," Jeb muttered. "Gate Control—" He broke off, as the sight of the hypergate coming at him like a mailed fist emptied his thoughts. "—this is *Ranger One*," he finished, his voice straining. "Engines will not respond. Require assistance. Repeat . . ."

West watched and listened, barely breathing; trapped in his best friend's worst nightmare and unable to wake up. A stranger's voice over the radio said, "*Ranger One*, this is Grissom Base. Rescue craft have been dispatched."

West shook himself out, angled his position until he could see three rescue ships streaking toward them.

"*Impact in sixty seconds . . .*"

They would be too late. He looked ahead again. The hypergate filled his vision; he could make out every detail of the scorched, twisted metal and the dangling entrails of ruptured lines where enemy fire or flying debris had found their marks. He opened his comm link. "Grissom, this is *Eagle One*. Those Pugs will never reach him in time."

"*Eagle One*," the radio spat, "clear this frequency, and return to base."

West hung motionless for a handful of heartbeats, staring down at his friend's ship, watching inertia's irresistible force sweep it toward the hypergate's immovable object.

"This is *Eagle One*. I'm going after him."

"Negative, *Eagle One*," the controller said sharply. "Your craft is not equipped—"

West hit his thrusters, sending his craft in a headlong dive toward Jeb's ship and the massive structure that was rising with unbelievable speed to meet them both.

"Impact in thirty seconds—"

A section of flaming debris exploded outward from the gate's surface and hurtled toward them. *Jeb's ship would never even survive long enough to hit the gate—*

West hit the firing stud, grinned in satisfaction as his lasers fragmented the massive chunk of debris and he watched it scatter harmlessly. He was still accelerating, closing faster all the time with Jeb's ship; his mind and the displays told him it still wasn't fast enough.

"What the *hell* are you doing?" Jeb's voice demanded suddenly, hurting his ears.

"Making balloon animals," West snapped. He could actually see Jeb in his harness now—the precise curve of his shaven skull, his dark face looking out in disbelief through the *Ranger's* transparent dome. "Saving your ass!" he hissed.

But the vast pockmarked surface of the gate was all that Jeb saw now, all that he could see—

"Major West!" the radio blared; West's jaw tightened. "You are not authorized to jeopardize this asset. Return to base. That is a *direct* order. Acknowledge—"

West slammed his hand down, shutting off the radio. "Never liked that station, anyway," he muttered, to the naked mass of twisted metal that was about to vaporize them both, ship and all. He was one with the ship again, dodging debris, blowing fragments of gate out of his path with a laser burst. Jeb's ship was directly below him now. He could almost reach out and grab it . . .

"Impact in five seconds—"

"Don, man," Jeb whispered, "I'm really scared . . ."

West pulled ahead at last, shooting past Jeb's fighter

as he drove his ship toward the wall of steel and alloy in an ever-steepening dive.

"*Warning, proximity alert—*"

"Jeb," West murmured, "I'm going to give you a little kiss. Don't take it the wrong way."

He dove past Walker's bow, blotting out Jeb's view of Armageddon with his fuselage.

"You're too close!" Jeb shouted frantically. "Abort. *Abort!*"

"Going up," West said, his voice inhumanly calm. His hands were white with tension as he angled the joystick up; his face was a mask of resolve so utter that he wouldn't have known it in a mirror.

Sandwiched between the gate's surface and Jeb's fighter, he jagged sharply upward; the *Eagle One*'s cockpit dome glanced off Walker's cockpit like a cue ball. *Eight ball in the side pocket.*

The kiss knocked Jeb's ship off course, through a flaming gap in the gate's surface where the attackers had scored a direct hit, and onward into clear space.

West's teeth gritted together over his wordless shout of elation as his own rebounding craft *skreel*ed across the surface of the hypergate, sending up a red-hot plume of shaven metal.

He goosed the thrusters; gasped in relief as the ship responded, arcing out and away from the gate's torn surface before he became the final statistic on its damage report.

"Does this mean we're going steady?" Jeb asked hoarsely.

West laughed; somehow his own voice held together

as he said, "You weren't getting out of buying those beers that easy."

He cut the thrusters, letting himself drift; watching the *Ranger One* until the rescue craft converged on it. Only when he was sure that Walker was safe did he put his own ship back on a trajectory toward Grissom Base.

Chapter One

The music swelled—heroic, triumphant, full of vio-
lins—its sound too large to be contained inside such a
tiny monitor; like the image of outer space incongruously downsized to fit a palm-wide vid screen.

Somber yet stirring, the voice-over intoned, *"Since the
dawn of history, men and women have searched for a land
of plenty, where unlimited resources are available to all . . ."*

The image on the screen became a windswept dream
couple—a handsome, bearded man and a dark-haired,
beautiful woman standing side by side. Their faces were
as familiar to the boy as his own hand cradling the monitor—and yet at the same time they were total strangers.
The sight of them always bothered and depressed him,
no matter how often he saw it.

*"This man, Professor John Robinson, inventor of the
faster-than-light hyperdrive, will make that timeless
dream a reality."*

The stylized blue-and-gold ovals of the Jupiter Mission logo flashed on the screen, framing the couple with
their three perfect children: a blond young woman, a
dark-haired girl, and a towheaded boy. They all wore
equally unnatural, digitally altered smiles.

"John Robinson and his family have been specially trained to make a ten-year journey across the galaxy in the world's most advanced spacecraft, the Jupiter . . ."

Abruptly they all winked out of existence, replaced by the dome of a towering launch apparatus gleaming in the early sun.

"The Robinson family will be the vanguard for generations of families to come. They will join our research colony on Alpha Prime. There they will become the first settlers on a world where unlimited food and water will be the birthright for all . . ."

The scene shifted to a satellite photo of a world that was clearly not Earth. *"Alpha Prime will be a new Eden. A chance for mankind to spread its wings across the galaxy."* A computer simulation swept the viewer down from orbit, giving the watching boy the eyes of a bird in flight, soaring over sun-dappled cropland rich with magnificent harvests. *"What kind of future can our children look forward to?*

"A future in paradise . . ."

The boy blinked as the vision of a new Eden was swept aside by a new logo—a corporate logo this time—and the incongruous sight of a Coke bottle hurtling toward the stars.

"This mission sponsored by the U.S. Army and the Coca-Cola Corporation."

Will Robinson, the blond-haired youngest child of "heroic Professor John Robinson," screwed his imperfect ten-year-old's face into an expression of hopeless disgust. "'*Coke,*'" he mimicked, echoing the narrator's final words, "'saving the future for our children.'" His free hand went to the pocket-sized computer resting in his palm. "Give me a break," he muttered, and activated a new program on his hacker's deck.

Peering out through the slats of the door, Will watched his mother morosely from his hiding place in the coat closet. Mom stood in the middle of the living room gesturing like a juggler, hand-signaling the movers what to take next as she simultaneously carried on a conversation with the pissed-off principal of his school. At least in his secret hiding place he was safe, for the moment, from the chaos that ruled his house and his life.

Maybe too safe . . . As he listened to the principal's voice rise, and saw the look on his mother's face, his hand moved to the keypad of his deck again.

"He hacked our main power grid to run his experiment," the principal was saying, waving her own hands. "The school was in chaos! We didn't even have lights."

The living room lights suddenly dimmed around her. The principal flickered too; she was only a holograph, an avatar of the real person. When her image solidified again, her virtual head had been grafted onto the iconic body of Arnold Schwarzenegger, his biceps rippling. She ranted on, oblivious to the sabotage.

Will contemplated his selection of other fantasy figures and grinned. "The changing shape of education . . ." he murmured, and set her head on the body of semi-emaciated supermodel Twiggy.

Outside in the living room, his mother laughed out loud. Will peered through the slats in time to see her look of chagrin as she realized the principal had no idea what was happening. Mom began to drift casually around the living room, surreptitiously glancing behind couches and into empty cabinets.

"This is no laughing matter, Professor Robinson," the principal said sharply. "Will is terribly gifted. His little time machines, though pure fancy, are the products of a truly brilliant mind."

Will frowned. Her body became an ape's.

Just then his mother yanked open the closet door. Light poured into his cramped hideout, exposing his covert activities. Will grinned up at her.

Mom shook her head, her expression stalled between aggravation and laughter. "No more monkey business," Mom said, as sternly as she could manage through the unproductive urge to smile back at him.

Will shrugged, and fiddled with his deck. Out in the living room the principal was suddenly herself again, still droning on, utterly oblivious.

"...but the boy is starved for attention. I know your life is anything but normal right now, but was there *no* way his father could have attended the science fair?"

Will sighed, and his smile disappeared.

John Robinson stared out the window of his office in the elevated dome of Houston Space Command, and sighed. The view from the thirty-story structure of the Jupiter Mission launch platform was panoramic, letting him see the vast urban sprawl of the Houston-Austin-Dallas megatropolis extending beyond even the horizon under a dark, wet sky. Immense industrial air purifiers drifted high above, like the bizarre ships of an invading alien armada.

If he turned 180 degrees, he would see the same sight, where Houston-Austin-Dallas merged imperceptibly into its sister city beyond the Mexican border. He glanced at his watch, wishing he could be anywhere else; wishing most of all that he could be home with his family, today of all days.

But he was doing this for his family. What he wanted right now wasn't important; what he wanted would have to wait.

"Professor Robinson—" The hundred separate voices all calling his name at once penetrated his thoughts by their sheer volume. "Can you confirm reports that Global Sedition attacked the hypergate last night? Is that why the mission has been pushed up?"

"Um . . . sorry?" John turned, tugging absently at his beard as he faced the monitor in front of him. A mob of reporters jostled for position on its screen. *All waiting to talk to him.*

The media had been given short notice about this much-hyped guided tour, which had been moved up along with everything else; but in spite of that, it didn't look like anyone at all had refused the invitation. The crowd was a living portrait of the human race: The varieties of skin color and hairstyles and clothing he saw among them reminded him that they had come from every part of the globe for this event—because if the Jupiter Mission succeeded, it would change the future of the entire world. *Because if it didn't, the world might not have a future . . .*

He shook his head, hoping that he only seemed to be clearing it, and not letting his subconscious express how he really felt about facing the relentless curiosity of billions of watchers. "Sorry, you'll have to ask the War Department. As far as I know, we're leaving tomorrow because celestial rotations have produced a preferable launch window."

The lie came out so smoothly that it shocked him, as if Media Relations had reprogrammed his brain without his knowing it, to match his digitally perfect image in their ads. It was a wonder anyone recognized him in a live broadcast.

"So, let's begin." He pressed on before anyone could badger him for nonexistent details. If he could just get their attention back on the mission itself, they might forget about the new launch date, at least until it had become a meaningless question.

The media were already on board *Jupiter*, ready to begin their tour. The crowd filled Engineering nearly to capacity—a sea of human faces dotted with the empty humanoid stares of the 3D/VR cams. Watchful ASOMAC guards ringed the crowd; the utilitarian black of their military uniforms made a pragmatic comment on the colorful excess of the media's streetwear. The plasma rifles they carried made a more pointed comment about any questionable behavior on the part of their guests.

Beyond the mob of reporters, John could see the stolid, gleaming drive technology of the nuclear-electrics, and the sleek, streamlined tech of the long-range fusion engines. Red-hatted technicians were running final systems checks on the banks of displays around the hyperdrive—the true heart of his lifelong dream.

"As you know," he said, slipping inside the speech he

now knew by rote, "Alpha Prime is the only habitable planet yet detected by Deep Space Recon. My crew will sleep away our ten-year journey there in suspended animation." *His crew—his family.* The surreal feeling that he had become two different men with the same name washed over him again. "Once we have rendezvoused with the research colony on Alpha, I will surpervise construction of a hypergate."

A computer-generated image of the hypergate appeared on the monitor's screen—what viewers everywhere were seeing now. He smiled at the vision of his infradimensional theorems made real.

He'd first had the idea that would lead to this moment when he was only a boy. He had spent the decades since then trying to make it work, first in computer simulation, and then in the far more unforgiving arena of outer space. Sometimes he had wondered if he would ever live long enough to see it through. He had almost given it up as futile, more than once.

It had been Maureen's faith in him, their love for each other and for their children, that had kept him believing in his dream of a better future—a dream that had come to include not just their own family, but all families ...

"By then, technicians here on Earth will have completed the companion hypergate in our planet's orbit." Now his words were matched to a visual of the gate already under construction in near-Earth space, the image enhanced by graphic overlays showing its completed form. "Once both gates are complete, ships will be able to pass instantaneously between them. Immediate colonization of Alpha Prime will be possible."

"Can't you just use the *Jupiter*'s hyperengine to zap straight to Alpha Prime?" another reporter asked.

Doesn't the press ever read the PR releases about this mission? He felt as if he had been answering these same questions endlessly, for years; wasting time that could have been spent working constructively on the project . . . or even spent at home with his wife and children. He swallowed his impatience, and said, "As you know, hyperspace exists 'beneath' normal space. If you try to enter hyperspace without a gate"—behind him the graphics produced a spaceship, positioned randomly in the corner of a turning schematic of the galaxy—"your exit vector is random. There's no telling where you'd come out. Ninety-eight percent of the galaxy is still uncharted. There's a lot of space to get lost in out there."

"Professor," someone else shouted, "how is Captain Daniels recovering from the flu? Will he still be able to pilot the mission?"

John glanced away. General Benjamin Hess, the military commander in charge of the project—and his father's longtime friend—stood silently in the doorway to his office, observing and listening to the interview. *Help me out here, Ben.*

Hess stepped forward as if on cue into the sight of the reporters onscreen. "Ladies and gentlemen, you came to get a look at the *Jupiter One*," he said, smiling. "Don't you think you've waited long enough?"

Relieved, John touched a button on his desk, and the room went dark. The immense display screen set up in his office specifically for this occasion came alive, showing the watching reporters an image of the launch area.

The enormous saucer-form ship rested on its launch pad, still firmly bound to the earth by a maze of gantries, fueling systems, and loading belts. Steam and venting gases shrouded it with ephemeral clouds.

"Professor"—some reporter asked, before he could escape—"how do your children feel about leaving Earth behind?"

John paused, and smiled. "They couldn't be more excited."

Chapter Two

"**This mission** *sucks!*" The voice of Penny Robinson, fourteen and furious, echoed down the stairwell of the Robinson family's large suburban colonial.

And probably all through the neighborhood, too, Maureen Robinson thought wearily, looking up the stairs at her screaming daughter.

Penny stood at the top, dressed in black from head to foot, as if she were in mourning; though Maureen knew that it was simply her preferred mode of dress. Her daughter's clothes and mood were the antithesis of the cheerful pastels Penny was always shown wearing in the computer-enhanced mission portraits, where the whole family looked like they had been extruded from a plastics factory.

"I don't want to leave early! I don't want to go at *all!*" Penny shouted, as if light-years separated them, instead of twenty-odd steps.

"We'll talk about this over dinner—" Maureen repeated, feeling by now as if she could have recited the words in her sleep, and probably had.

Penny clenched her fists, still shouting, "For the last three years I have missed *everything*, training so I can spend the next ten years missing everything else! I am *not* staying home for dinner. I am going out to see my *friends*. I am going to say *good-bye* to my *entire life!*"

"Penny," Maureen struggled to keep her tone firm and even, to keep the same kind of anger and exasperation out of it. "I need you home tonight." She shook her head.

Penny glared daggers at her mother, shaking her own head as she retreated into the shadows of the hallway. Mom stood unmoving and unmoved at the bottom of the stairs, guarding the front door like an ogre.

Penny turned and stormed off down the hall, fighting tears as she activated her cam/watch. "On the eve before she is torn from all she knows," she dictated, "kidnapped, hurled into deep space against her will, what thoughts fill the mind of the young Space Captive . . . ?"

She passed the doorway to her own room and barged uninvited into the bedroom of her younger brother.

Will looked up with a scowl of annoyance. He stood in the middle of a sea of toys and science experiments, holding onto a single empty packing canister, the last one labled PERSONAL CARGO. The posters on his walls, the CDs in their rack, the lab equipment on his shelves . . . even the replica of a Great White shark's head and the weird green thing with the lizard hanging from his ceiling . . . were still untouched.

He looked, she thought, like someone being forced to abandon ship, trying to choose which precious items from all his worldly goods he would take with him. Which, in a way, he was.

"'Will there be *boys* on Alpha Prime?'" Will said theatrically, talking through his nose as he tried to mimic her voice. "'What will I *wear*?'"

She glared at him. Then she looked down at her cam/watch. "In the future," she said, "the video journals of Penny Robinson, Space Captive, will be devoured by millions. I will be world famous." She looked back at her brother. "You, on the other hand, will be totally forgotten." Will frowned.

Penny resumed her narrative, satisfied. Holding the camcorder out where it could scan her other arm, she recorded the black sleeve of her shirt, which was adorned with ribbons from wrist to shoulder. "The Space Captive has decided to wear ribbons of support for fellow sufferers, green for ecological issues, white for human rights—"

"Wait until your arm drops off from lack of circulation," Will said sullenly.

Penny ignored him. Shutting off her cam, she began to rummage in the packed boxes sitting along the wall. She found a vacuum-sealed bundle and lifted it out. "I wonder what it'll be like to jettison your body into deep space . . . ?" She turned back to him, fixing him with an ominous gaze. "First you'll try holding your breath. But your blood's already begun to boil. Then your skin inflates like a balloon. And *pop*! Space soup."

Will's face wrinkled up like a prune. "Do they have a *name* for what's wrong with you?" he said.

Penny pulled one of several palm-sized, gold-plated stars out of the crate, and turned it over in her hand to read the inscription: FIRST PRIZE. They all said "first prize." *Probably for Best Nerd*, she thought. Her brother had no life. Using a sharp-edged arm of the medal, she deftly slashed open the plastic on the mystery bundle. She handed the star to Will.

"Dad says don't bring them . . ." Will said, looking down. He tossed the medal aside like a used tissue. "Like *anything* I do matters to him."

Penny felt a sudden pang of empathy. The same thought had been in her mind lately more often than she could count. "Don't sweat it, kid," she said casually, trying to snap them both out of their mood. "I got videos for two birthdays, and he forgot last year *completely*." She reached out to give him a brief hug. "This mission is the only thing he cares about anymore." She stepped back, unwrapping and uncoiling her mystery bundle: the mesh ladder she had hidden here for exactly this situation. She tossed it out the open window and got ready to climb down.

Will looked on in amazement, surprised by the hug as much as by his sister's resourcefulness. "So, that's a *no* to family dinner?"

Penny turned back, giving him the usual pained expression. "Let's see," she said, tapping her forehead. "Do I spend my last night on Earth watching Mom and Dad pretend not to be fighting again, or blow ten years worth of allowance at the mall . . . you do the math." She turned away again and put a leg over the windowsill. Her foot thumped the siding on the outer wall, searching for a rung of the ladder.

Will grimaced. "Mom's gonna go thermal."

Penny laughed. "What's she gonna do? *Ground* me?"

She swung her other leg over the sill. Inch by inch she disappeared downward, until all he could see in the window's frame was the summer dusk.

Will stood shaking his head, where way too many thoughts and feelings lay tangled inside his brain. His sister always seemed to be off in some imaginary world, making up adventures starring herself. He'd told Mom that Penny should become a writer; then she could be lost there all the time, and still make a living. The sooner she left home, the better *he'd* like it.

But now here they were, *all* leaving home; and they didn't even have any choice. Suddenly he could barely swallow because of the lump in his throat. No wonder Penny was acting out her daydreams: *real life had become totally unreal*. He kneeled down again, and went back to sorting toys.

Chapter Three

John Robinson walked beside General Hess down the echoing metal corridor of Space Command headquarters, wondering whether he would still see metal corridors when he closed his eyes tonight to sleep. He had seen them every previous night . . .

"Did all the preflight checks show ready?" Hess asked him.

John glanced up. "Ready as we can be," he said, a little irritably. "We've pushed this mission up three months, Ben."

"We're lucky those reporters didn't press us on Daniels's condition," Hess murmured, staring straight ahead, as if John's answers were not really of any significance.

John suddenly wondered whether Hess slept with his eyes open. "I'm worried about jamming in a new pilot at the last second," he said, pressing his argument more insistently. *You're putting my family at risk.* But he didn't say that.

"The Global Sedition is getting brave. They're not just renegade terrorist factions any more," Hess said, as if that was all the response his concern needed. "First the hypergate. Then Daniels. Next time, they may attack the launch dome. We can't afford to wait."

John didn't answer, knowing there was no point. He knew how Hess's mind worked—just like his father's had: *Duty first. The big picture . . .* He also knew how a career officer, focusing on constant threats of war, could find his definition of "the big picture" getting progressively narrower.

John had access to the same information—most of it classified—that Hess did. And there was something else he had learned from his father: how to read a report in which the real truth lay hidden between the lines. The Global Sedition was too well-equipped, too well organized, to be simply a "terrorist supergroup"—there were even rumors that they were secretly constructing their own hypergate. Terrorists were extremists. The idea that they would cooperate with other extremists of a different sociopolitical stripe was highly unlikely.

He was sure something subtler, and more dangerous, lay behind the attacks on this mission. Something like a conspiracy of multinationals—the vastly powerful, internationally based corporations that had made fortunes stripping the natural resources and exploiting the people of all but the richest nations; whose uncontrollable greed had left their homeworld all but unhabitable.

Who might be looking to the stars for future profits.

It was a scenario he found much easier to believe; especially when a multinational corporation already had the resources to co-fund the *Jupiter*'s voyage to Alpha Prime.

Whoever was behind the sabotage, he wasn't going to

let them win. Not when the hypergate might be the last chance for the survival of every living thing on Earth. He thought of his family again, of all they were sacrificing . . . of how much he loved them. *Too much to leave them behind . . .*

And as he thought of them, a nagging, misplaced memory surfaced in his brain. "Damn!" he said out loud. "Will's science fair." He activated the memo function on his watch. "Reminder: apology video for Will."

"He'll understand." The General glanced at him with a smile and a lift of his eyebrows.

John forced a smile in return, answering Hess's unspoken question. But the smile never touched his eyes. He looked away again. "I agree a military presence may be necessary now, Ben. But my family's on this mission. I need a pilot who's more than just spit and polish—"

"I've got your man," Hess said confidently. He stopped, pressing his palm against an ID panel. "He just doesn't know it yet." A door hissed open, revealing an empty conference room.

Not quite empty. A lone figure waited by the windows on the far side of the room, staring out at the darkening sky. Something about the way he stood made John think of a bird of prey trapped in a cage.

The man turned as he heard them enter, and saluted smartly. He wore a major's eagles, and an ASOMAC patch with the name WEST, on the black leather jacket of his duty uniform.

Brown hair, blue eyes, medium build . . . the only remarkable thing John could see about Major West was that the man was young enough to be his son. He found the thought depressing.

Hess returned the salute. "At ease, Major."

West's mouth opened even before his hand fell away to his side, as if he had been holding back a flood of words by sheer willpower. "Sir, why was I pulled off active duty? Those cybertechs may attack again. I need to be *up* there—"

"Do you know Professor Robinson?" the General asked, not even seeming to register West's agitation.

West stood blinking for a moment, nonplussed. He pulled himself together with an effort that was obvious to John, and said evenly, "By reputation only." He met John's gaze, and admiration shone in his eyes. "Your father's battle strategies were required reading at the Academy."

John bent his head in acknowledgment, and felt a bemused smile turn up the corners of his mouth. There was a time—a *long* time—when he had resented the reach of his father's inescapable shadow. But now, after the unrelenting media blitz of recent months, it was almost a relief to meet someone who only thought of him as his father's son.

"What can you tell me about the Jupiter Mission, Major?" Hess asked.

West barely controlled a frown. "The *Jupiter* is an oversized robot. Everything's automatic. It's a babysitting job, sir." He took a deep breath. "Any monkey in a flight suit can pilot the ship out of the solar system and set her down on Alpha Prime. No offense." He glanced at John again.

"Major," Hess said, with a touch of annoyance, "you *are* aware Earth's resources are severely limited."

West's forehead creased. "Permission to speak freely, sir?"

"Granted," the General said.

"Every schoolchild knows our recycling technologies will cure the environment." His hands rose from his sides, gesturing with barely controlled frustration. "Sending a family across the galaxy is a publicity stunt to sell soda to people of all ages!"

"Every schoolchild has been lied to," John said quietly. "Our really effective recycling technologies came too late. All fossil fuels are virtually exhausted. Fusion power may never be affordable enough for widespread use, and overreliance on solar power creates unpredictable atmospheric conditions. The ozone layer is down to forty percent. In two decades Earth will be unable to support human life."

West stared at him.

"The Global Sedition knows the truth as well as we do," the General said heavily. "They are building their own hypergate, and hope to colonize Alpha Prime first. If they are successful, they will not be inviting the world's population to join them across the galaxy. 'Western Demons' like you and I will be left on Earth to die."

John studied the floor. He'd heard that speech too often around here; had heard ones too much like it endlessly from his father, back during the millennial wars. It had never made sense to him. But over time he had come to recognize it as a kind of bigotry; and bigotry was never rational . . .

The hypergate he had envisioned was being built to serve all of Earth, and no one had ever even implied otherwise. It seemed to him that only the kind of short-sighted profiteers who had ruined the Earth's ecosystem would see sabotaging this mission as a good idea. And only a cartel of multinationals would have the resources to build a hypergate of its own . . . He glanced up again, into a lengthening silence.

". . . Captain Daniels doesn't have the flu, does he?" West said, at last.

Hess shook his head. "Daniels was murdered in his apartment last night. The flu story is a cover we fed the press."

West looked stunned. "I knew Daniels . . ." His blue eyes turned glacial. "We should pulse-blast their bases. A decisive strike—"

"Your rescue stunt in orbit was foolhardy." The General verbally cut him off at the knees. "Explain yourself, Major."

West straightened his shoulders, and there was no uncertainty in his voice as he said, "I had a friend in trouble."

"You endangered a ten-billion-dollar spacecraft, disobeyed a *direct order*, because of a friend?" Hess demanded.

"Yes, sir," West said, clearly unrepentant. "I did. Sir."

"He'll do," John said, and his own smile surprised him.

Hess smiled, just as suddenly. "Congratulations, Major, you're the new pilot of the Jupiter Mission."

West's face flushed with betrayal, not pleasure. "But,

sir," his voice veered dangerously close to real anger, "the fight is *here—*"

"You go tomorrow," the General said, as oblivious to West's protest as he was to anything that did not fit neatly into his own preset vision. "Before the Sedition has a chance to ground this mission permanently. Let's go take a look at your ship."

Chapter Four

Dr. Zachary Smith stood at the peak of a windswept dune, gazing outward. Desert surrounded him on every side, for as far as he could see; the sand sea rippled with waves of heat under a ceramic blue dome of sky. A small, precise man with a neatly trimmed goatee, he was the kind of person others tended to see as competent but unremarkable. They could not have been more wrong.

Smith looked back at his companion impatiently; he was growing parched. "I was contracted to provide Daniels's apartment code," he said. "Nothing more. My work is done."

The anonymous well-dressed businessman at his side frowned. "They found a replacement pilot. The mission is going ahead on schedule. We require more direct intervention on your part."

A *replacement*. *Really*. Smith suppressed a sigh. "I see," he said. He knew these interchangeable corporate lackeys were simply ambulatory cash machines. But it depressed him to think that even the nameless board members who sent them to him had no idea of how the military actually functioned. There seemed to be nothing *but* pilots anymore; pilots were as plentiful as cockroaches. "Well, more direct intervention will cost you," he said pleasantly. "And I'm afraid my price has just become . . . astronomical."

The sound of knocking reached him from somewhere beyond the sky; as if its deep and perfect blue really was a ceramic bowl. Smith reached out, feeling in the air for something he couldn't see. He pressed a button.

The virtual businessman and the holographic desert scene vanished like a dream. "Room lights," Smith said wearily. The sudden return of brightness revealed his familiar laboratory at Mission Control, and the door across the room, on which someone had actually knocked. "Come in."

The door hissed open and a technician entered. "Control hasn't received the results of your preflight exams, Dr. Smith."

Smith crossed the room to the circular overhead light board, around which were displayed the faces of the *Jupiter*'s crew. *Like targets*, he thought. He smiled as he removed the microfiles and handed them to the technician. "The Robinsons are checked out at one hundred percent. They are in perfect condition, and ready to save the world." His smile widened, and the technician smiled happily back at him, never suspecting. "Wish them luck for me."

Don West followed the general and the professor along the gantryway that gave access to the *Jupiter*'s interior. Its vast saucer form loomed above him, making him feel even smaller and more powerless than the General's words already had. Its entry hatch lay waiting to swallow him up like a gaping mouth. He estimated that the *Jupiter*'s holds could accommodate a hundred ships like the *Eagle One* easily.

"The mission protocols are simple," Hess was saying. "Professor Robinson is in command, unless you encounter a combat situation. In that case, Major West, you will assume command."

That civilian—? Don looked up, stricken. *The only space Robinson had ever flown through was the space between his ears.* He swallowed a fresh lump of his pride and tried again to get the General to listen to him. "I'm a fighter pilot, sir. There *must* be better candidates—"

They had reached the entry hatch. Hess turned to him and said, "Welcome aboard, Major." He and Robinson went on in without hesitation.

Why didn't they just court-martial me? Don thought, following glumly. They walked along a corridor that glowed with recessed lighting until they reached the closed blast doors at its far end. Don faced the others as they waited for the doors to open, and tried one last time to make them listen.

"Jeb Walker is a far better pilot, sir," he said. *Well, maybe not; but probably as good a pilot . . .* And Walker would jump at the chance to do something like this; Jeb thought the hypergate was the greatest thing since wings. "He'd be perfect for this mis—"

He broke off as the doors parted behind him. He turned, looking through them. His eyes widened. "Wow!" he breathed, suddenly ten years old again.

He entered the *Jupiter*'s bridge unthinkingly, reverently; the way he would have entered heaven. That was what this was, he thought: *high-tech heaven*. Two pilot seats with state-of-the-art cyberware faced an enormous expanse of viewport; its flawless curve was made of the same transparent alloy as his ship's cockpit, he supposed, although his mind persisted in imagining it was window glass. Technicians moved here and there around the room, performing systems checks.

He scoped out the helm; appraised the working CPU; studied the displays on the navigation pedestal in the center of the room. He checked monitors and equipment and screens. He was definitely impressed.

"Looks like somebody sprung for the full extras package on this baby," he murmured, more to himself than to the two men observing him.

"If you have to baby-sit, it's not such a bad nursery; wouldn't you agree, Major?" Robinson asked encouragingly.

Don looked up at him, glanced away again as a tech emerged from behind the cryo sleep array he hadn't even gotten to yet: a doctor of some kind, dressed in pragmatic maroon coveralls and carrying a clipboard. A woman doctor. An extremely attractive woman doctor. Don stared, as nature hit the reset button in his brain for the second time in as many minutes.

"I don't get it." Her attention was on Robinson and the General, as if she hadn't even noticed him. "I can't get the cryo sleep systems up over ninety-six percent."

"Doctor Smith approved the specs—" General Hess began.

"Doctor Smith is base physician," she snapped, cutting him off. "I am responsible, once this ship is in flight. These tubes will be perfect or this ship will not launch. Is that clear?"

"Absolutely, Doctor," Hess said, chastened.

Oh, my God, Don thought, *I think I'm in love.*

"Judy," Robinson said, as she began to turn away, "I'd like you to meet Major West. He's taking Mike's place."

The doctor—Judy—turned back, seeming actually to notice him for the first time. She put out her hand, and Don shook it. Her blond hair was pulled back in a simple knot that only accented her perfect cheekbones, and her eyes were green. They widened slightly as she looked him up and down and up again; she seemed to be enjoying the view. Her gaze rose to his face, lingered on his mouth . . . met his own eyes staring back at her.

Her cheeks reddened as she realized he'd caught her checking him out. He grinned, letting her know the admiration was mutual.

"He's heavier than Mike," she said, abruptly turning back to Robinson. "We'll have to recalibrate."

"I'd be happy to discuss my dimensions, Doctor..." Don put on his best roguish smile, the one that invariably worked. "Say, over dinner?"

"West . . ." Judy looked at him again. "I've read about you. You're a war hero, aren't you?"

"Well, yes, actually," he said, preening.

She folded her arms, resting her chin on her palm. "Who was it who said, 'Those who can't think, fight'? . . . Oh. *Me.*" Her smile turned to cryo freeze. "Well, nice to have met you." She walked away, heading back toward the cryo units.

"That's one cold fish *I'd* love to thaw." Don glanced knowingly at the other two men, trying to disguise his embarrassment with a smirk.

Across the room, Judy looked up again. Her gaze grazed him, and then settled pointedly on Robinson. "I'm not going to make it over for dinner, Dad," she said.

Don turned to stare at Robinson: *Dad—?* Robinson raised his eyebrows; shrugged, smiling.

This had to be a bad dream. Don shut his eyes, wondering when he was going to wake up. He opened them, and everyone was looking at him. He swore under his breath. "It's going to be a long flight," he muttered.

Chapter
Five

It was so late by the time John got home that he couldn't bring himself to look at his watch. As he got out of the car, he saw the lights still on everywhere in the house. They were like a beacon in the darkness as he started up the front path, reminding him of why everything he'd done, everything he'd given up in the way of a normal life, mattered so much.

He entered the house, glancing right and left. Everyone must have gone to bed long ago, he supposed. He went into the dining room; stopped, as he saw the remains of an elegant dinner on the table—the candles unlit, the food never eaten. Their last dinner, on their last night on Earth . . . and he hadn't been home for it.

John crossed the room slowly to look at something else sitting on the table. Will's science project. Another gold-plated first prize star hung from a ribbon around its base. He smiled. Will was so much like he'd been when he was a boy . . .

Maureen got up out of bed as she heard her husband enter the house. She had been lying awake waiting for that sound for far too long, after getting to bed far too late. Her first response was relief that he was finally home; but she knew that wouldn't last. It never did.

She put on her robe and started down the stairs, reminding herself to stay calm, to discuss things logically, to try not to— She saw John standing beside the dining room table, looking at Will's science project.

Behind him she saw the beautiful dinner she had prepared so stubbornly and lovingly, giving in to her fantasy that the whole family would sit down together for once, this one last time, to eat their last meal in their own home, on their own planet . . . She hadn't had the time, she hadn't had the energy to spare; but she had done it anyway, because what it symbolized had been so important to her.

And then the only one who had even been home to eat it was Will—and Will had been angry and hurt because John had broken his promise about the science fair again. Will had refused to eat anything, saying he didn't *like* fried chicken, he had *never* liked fried chicken, before running off to his room and slamming the door. And somehow, after that, she hadn't felt like eating either.

"He won first prize again," she said, as John looked up at her.

"A nonworking prototype for his time machine," John said, with a cheerful smile that didn't work either. "Sharp stuff for a midget."

She just looked at him, clutching the edges of her robe in a death grip.

John looked away from her expression, and his

pasted-on smile disappeared. "I'm sorry about dinner. The new pilot . . ."

She took a deep breath. "John, the family needs you here—"

"This mission is *about* our family," he said, his voice rising to drown hers out. "My only condition for taking this mission was that we could bring the children with us! So doing our job wouldn't mean leaving them behind. So future generations will have a new home—"

"We can't compete, John!" She heard her own voice rising, unable to stop herself. "You're off saving humanity! So what does it matter that Will has to black out his school just to get his father's attention? That Penny got dragged home by security for the third night in a row. Or that Judy's become a ghost, just like her father—?"

"Maureen, I'm trying to compensate for the new launch time—"

"What do you think I'm doing!" she shouted. "Throwing *Tupperware parties*?"

John spread his hands in useless apology. "I *know* you're revising the life science protocols. I meant—"

"I'm also trying to handle two kids who are leaving an entire *planet* behind! There are no *books* on how to deal with this!" She pushed her hair back from her eyes. She'd been an Army brat, growing up: She knew how to move a family; she knew about discipline and hard work and making sacrifices. For years now she had juggled the demands of family and career; it had never been easy, but the stress had always seemed worth it, because she loved them both so much. But *this*— She turned away, hugging herself, her eyes brimming.

John moved close to her, rested his hands on her shoulders. "And maybe it doesn't do any good to save a world of families, if we can't save our own?" he asked gently. "Is that it, Professor?"

Slowly, Maureen turned back to face her husband. She smiled, tentatively at first; as she looked up into his eyes her smile grew warm and real. "I told my mother she was wrong about you," she whispered, her voice still a little shaky. Suddenly remembering her mother, missing her, Maureen looked away again, out the window. "Why did we make the Earth sick? John, I'm—" *So afraid*. Afraid to say it.

"I know, baby," he whispered. He closed her in his arms as if they were young lovers again; he hadn't called her that in years. "I'm scared too."

They went upstairs together, passing the children's rooms one by one. John hesitated at Will's doorway, then stepped inside. Maureen watched him move along the pathway of light from the hall to his son's bedside.

John's hand rose to the dog tags hanging on a chain around his neck: his father's dog tags. John had kept them for his father whenever he was away, which had been most of the time, during the millennial wars. It had been the Old Man's promise to his son: that he would always come home . . .

And then, one time, he didn't.

John always wore the tags, as a reminder of his loss; as a reminder of his vow not to repeat his father's mistakes. As a reminder of how much his family meant to him. It was one of the things that she loved about him.

He stood for a long moment looking down at Will.

Will lay peacefully asleep, the way they all should have been. Maureen hoped that her son's dreams on this final night were sweet ones.

At last John left Will's bedside and rejoined her in the hall. They walked on, hand in hand, to their own waiting bedroom, and she turned out the final light.

The lights would burn all night at Space Command, as the hours until launch silently bled away. The *Jupiter One* stood sleepless amid its loading gantries, as the final supplies rolled into its cargo holds on automated lifts and conveyer belts.

The human workers pulling an all-nighter were too preoccupied even to look twice at the cargo drum labeled BIOLOGICAL MATERIALS: DO NOT OPEN, let alone consider violating its warning. They hoisted it by crane, deposited it in the assigned storage area, and left it there.

Smith waited until the space around the cargo drum was utterly silent again before he forced the lid and climbed out, cursing his cramped muscles and their inability to function without pain. He looked back at the cargo container in distaste, before he scanned the room for the access panel he knew would be here somewhere. His eyes found it, exactly where he had been told it would be.

His interrupted negotiations with the Anonymous Businessman had been resolved in a very satisfactory manner. When he finished this last, unpleasantly personal act of betrayal, he would be rich beyond anyone's dreams; anyone's except, perhaps, his own. What was his dignity, compared to that? He had lost far more than his dignity in the past. He pulled open the access panel and climbed in.

Money and death were the only constants left, in a universe where Professor John Robinson had made it possible to get around the speed of light. They were certainly the only things with any meaning for him. After this one final act of sabotage, he planned to disappear, and spend the rest of his life in some idyllic hideaway. What did it matter to him if he doomed the world? He wouldn't be around to see it.

Self-anointed saviors like Robinson made him want to vomit. They deserved to die, along with their simplistic dreams. It was simply an added bonus that his would be the hand to prove how truly meaningless Robinson and his perfect family were to the universe at large.

Smith peered out through grate after grate on the lower level, searching for the area of the ship he needed to see. *Getting closer.* He imagined the smiling faces of the Robinsons spread across every news monitor in the world, as the failure of the Jupiter Mission was announced. *How shocking. How terrible . . .* He smiled.

And then the abyss opened inside him, and swallowed even that ephemeral moment of satisfaction.

He had believed that if only he could amass enough money, it would fill the empty pit where his soul had been. He realized now that there was not enough money in the universe.

Well, maybe spending it all will work, he thought bitterly. He had a brilliant mind; everyone said so. He should be able to think of some truly creative ways to amuse himself . . . He peered out into yet another open space, this time seeing the one he expected. He slid open the service panel and eased himself into the robot bay.

This room was dimly lit by service lights, like all the others; annoying, but sufficient for his purposes.

He crossed to the main computer console, glancing right and left, listening for an unexpected footstep. It struck him as ironic that the only thing he profoundly cared about was his own survival . . . ironic, because his life was completely without pleasure.

Smith withdrew the small keypad from its housing on the chest panel of his field suit. He jacked into a dormant CPU panel and activated the override program. "You'll forgive me if I forgo the kiss, my sleeping behemoth," he murmured. "But the time has come to wake." He hit a glowing button on the display panel, and system indicators blinked to life. He input his first command.

The monotonal voice of the main computer bank responded, *"Robot is online. Reviewing primary directives: One, preserve the Robinson family. Two, maintain ship systems. Three—"*

"*Spare* me the chatter, my steely centurion." Smith's mouth twisted; his fingers rapped the keypad impatiently and the synthesized voice cut off. "Sadly, I fear I have far more dire deeds in store for you." He input the reprogramming commands and hit the button again.

"*Robot is online,*" the unnervingly flat voice repeated. "*Reviewing primary directives: Sixteen hours into mission, destroy Robinson family. Destroy all systems.*"

"Now that's more like it." He smiled, unjacking the keypad and reattaching it to his suit. "Farewell, my platinum-plated pal. Parting is such sweet sorrow—" He sent the robot a mocking salute, where it waited in a shadowed alcove across the room. "Give my regards to oblivion."

He left the control panel and made his way to a chute marked WASTE DISPOSAL. *How appropriate,* he thought. He climbed inside and began crawling downward. According to his source, it would let him exit the ship in a spot where he would be able to slip away unnoticed.

He had only gone a short way when the programming module attached to his coveralls began to beep. He activated its built-in comm link, his hands clumsy with sudden nerves. The face of the Nameless Businessman appeared in the air above him.

"Apparently you have completed your mission on schedule," his contact said, glancing around. "I do so admire a good spot of timely terrorism."

Smith might have enjoyed the floating head's attempt at droll humor, under other circumstances. But its presence here was endangering his life. "I told you *never* to call me," he hissed. "The transmission could be traced—"

The holographic face looked unconcerned. "I just wanted to express my most sincere gratitude for your unflagging loyalty," the Businessman said. "Good work, good Doctor. And good-bye." He smiled.

Smith frowned, puzzled, as the Businessman's smiling

face disappeared. The reprogramming module began to emit a sound so high-pitched that it hurt his ears.

And then there was real pain, as the rapidly overheating module burned its way through the coveralls' equipment shell. Smith ripped the keypad free from its housing, cursing as it seared his palm.

Before he could hurl it away, the overloaded module discharged. Agony lit up every cell of his spasming body, as the charge passed through him to ground itself in the passageway's metal floor.

The chute was silent again; as silent as a tomb. Zachary Smith lay very, very still within it.

Chapter Six

The Space Command complex seemed to shine with the light of hope in the dawn of an uncommonly bright new day.

Inside the launch area, within the bridge of *Jupiter One*, the Robinson family made their final preparations for a decade-long sleep under Judy's watchful eye. Will and Penny entered their cryogenic chambers first, wearing the gunmetal-and-silver protective suits that, Penny archly declared, made them look like they'd been wrapped in aluminum foil for their stay in the freezer.

More like seeds, sleeping in silver seed pods . . . Maureen thought, as she glanced up at the cryo unit surrounding Penny. She pushed the image out of her mind. Smiling at her fidgety daughter, she gently brushed the untidy strands of dark hair away from her beautiful brown eyes.

"Don't, Mom!" Penny said, brushing them forward again irritably. "*Vogue* says this will be the style in ten years."

Maureen took her hand away obediently, respecting her children's efforts to keep their spirits up; knowing how hard it was, for all of them.

"Can we cut back on her oxygen a little," Will asked, from the next cryo chamber, "so she's not quite so *annoying* when she wakes up?"

"Does *he* have to wake up at *all*?" Penny shot back.

"That's it!" Maureen tried to frown, and laughed instead. "I'm turning this spaceship right around!... Sleep good, babies," she said softly, as she had said to them every night at bedtime when they were very small. She kissed them on the forehead, also part of that long-ago ritual, before stepping back to let John take his turn.

When he reached Will, John put out his arms for a hug . . . just as Will tried to shake his hand. Father and son gazed at each other in awkward embarrassment before Will backed into his tube, resigned. John ruffled Will's hair and moved away. Maureen stepped into her own cryo unit, waiting as John came to her side. "You get a C in paternal expression, Professor," she said softly. "But an A for effort."

John kissed her smiling lips.

She sighed, and touched his face. "You always get an A in that."

John smiled too, and stepped inside his own unit. "Major," he called to Don West, "she's all yours."

Don looked up and nodded, canceling the redundant ops program he had been running from the *Jupiter*'s command console. He had put all the systems through their final preflight checks, trying to make himself as unobtrusive as possible while the Robinsons settled in for their ten-year sleep.

Face-to-face with the actual Robinson family, he found that he couldn't go on seeing them as some kind of animated publicity stunt. They were real people, and even if they were crazy to be doing this, he knew they deserved a privacy his outsider's presence made impossible. And as he watched them together, realizing the kind of trust they had in each other . . . what kind of love it took, to face what they were doing . . . he felt more like an outsider than ever.

He hadn't wanted to see any more, after that. It only reminded him of how much he didn't want to be here; and how, unlike the Robinsons, he had absolutely no choice in the matter.

But now he turned to look at them again, not having any choice about that either. "I'll try to give you a smooth ride" was all he could think of to say. John Robinson nodded and smiled, and so he supposed it must have been enough.

Judy Robinson walked down the line of cryo tubes, saying good-bye to her family one more time as she attached their bio monitors. At last she came to her own tube, waiting at the end of the row, and entered it. "Mission Control, this is Dr. Robinson. We are in the green."

The voice of Mission Control answered from the com console behind him: "Roger, Doctor, you are go to initiate cryostasis."

Impulsively, Don crossed the room. "One question, Doctor," he said stopping in front of her. "Is there room in these tubes for two?"

Her expectant gaze became a wall. "Barely enough

for you and your ego, Major." Her voice flash-froze him where he stood.

Don turned away, kicking himself mentally. Every time he got near her, his brain seemed to reverse polarities and turn him into an idiot. *All he had wanted was not to feel so alone* ...

He stopped, suddenly recognizing the emotion he'd glimpsed deep in her eyes, before they had shut him out. He turned back to her and said, almost gently, "Don't sweat it, Doc. I do this all the time." He gestured at the control room, the ship around them.

Judy nodded, and her face eased into a look of gratitude. "Just drive carefully," she said, and a smile finally touched her lips.

Lucky smile, he thought. Maybe if he'd had a family like hers, growing up, instead of one he couldn't wait to get away from, he'd know how to act around her.

Judy reached toward the cryo freeze control panel and pressed one last stud. Don stepped back, watching the biopads on her suit lock into place and the protective shield slip across her eyes. The same thing was happening all down the line, as the windowed shells of the cryopods rotated shut over the Robinsons . . . as the glimmering frost of the cryo fields engulfed them in sudden blizzard, hiding them from his sight.

When the pod doors cleared again, Judy gazed out at him through the frost-dimmed glass, unblinking, unseeing, like a fairy-tale princess under a high-tech spell . . . locked in suspended animation. The cryo tubes began to rise slowly toward the chambers in the hull above him, where they would remain until it was time to wake.

He took a deep breath, and crossed the silent bridge to take his own place at the com. "Mission Control, this is *Jupiter One*. The Robinsons are all tucked in. We are ready to fly."

The voice of Noah Freeman, the head of Mission Control, was music to his ears as it broke the silence around him, "You are at T-minus ten minutes, and counting."

Don put the transmission on visual, and smiled.

Freeman and his crew of technicians appeared on the monitor, looking just the way he remembered them from his hurried tour of Space Command: like chaos in motion. Noah grinned, sliding into place before his console; he was even more disheveled than yesterday, if that was possible.

A couple of technicians waved, shouting, "Hey, Don!" Around them, banks of monitors gave them access to every significant detail of the *Jupiter's* status. A long view of the launch area and the ship occupied the enormous central screen covering an entire wall of Mission Control. He could see his own face among the multiple views.

Noah's crew had struck Don's military-trained eyes with the impact of a thrown pie as he met them yesterday: a bunch of gum-chewing, funky weirdos, wearing the most bizarre assortment of clothing he had ever seen outside of a thrift shop.

But as he met them individually, talked with them, let them show him their equipment, he remembered that they were all there for just one reason: they were the best at what they did. He had begun to see nerd chic as a different sort of uniform, proclaiming their unique identity.

Now, as he did his final systems checks and the final minutes counted down, he found the company of Noah's crew oddly reassuring.

"You are at T-minus one minute, and counting," Noah said, giving him a thumbs-up from a monitor screen.

His other monitors showed him exterior views of the ship, of gantries retracting and equipment lines disengaging. Overhead, the immense dome began to open.

"Powering main drive system," Don said. He felt the *Jupiter* come alive around him, as if the ship itself was trembling with eagerness to be under way.

"Major, your escape vector is clear of all traffic. Op is go on your command," Noah said, his eyes intent now on his own console.

"Roger, Houston," Don said. His hand hovered over the glowing control panel. *Ten years.* He was about to erase ten years of his life, for a job any well-trained monkey could do. "The monkey flips the switch," he muttered, and activated the drive.

The *Jupiter One* lifted off, rising into the sky, thundering toward the black edge of space. Don shut his eyes as the g-forces crushed him down into his seat, emptying his mind of regrets and everything else; until at last the *Jupiter* left Earth's gravity well behind, soaring effortlessly through the blackness as the engines ceased their burn. His thoughts fell back into logical patterns, even as his body drifted against its restraining straps, free of gravity's hold.

"*Jupiter One* . . ." Noah's voice filled his ears as he

shook himself out. "You are clear of Earth's atmosphere." He heard a cheer go up in the control room, and fumbled for a smile.

He input the command that would jettison the booster engines and the outer shielding. The ship shuddered as the explosive bolts blew. He watched his monitors as the cumbersome shields that had protected the *Jupiter*'s second stage during their nuclear-electric ascent drifted clear.

On his screens now, like a butterfly newly emerged from a chrysalis, was the *Jupiter Two*: the state-of-the-art interstellar craft that would make the actual journey to Alpha Prime. He had never seen anything like the artistry of its design, the technological grace of its spired, ovate hull. It was beautiful . . . despite the fact that it was taking him away from everything that mattered.

"*Jupiter One* booster disengaged," he said. "Proceeding toward Mercury." He activated the *Jupiter Two*'s drive. The fusion engines came alive, glowing with atomic fire, and the artificial gravity of the ship's acceleration dropped him down into his seat again. He checked the displays and enabled the preprogrammed coordinates that would guide the ship's course inward toward the sun. *Damn milk run*, he thought, disgusted.

He watched the Earth fall away, along with all trace of humanity's tentative interface with the universe: satellites; zero gravity manufacturing stations; even the obsolete orbiting billboards that were still visible from the planet's surface on rare semiclear days. The hypergate and Stargate City . . . his entire life. *God, he'd never even told Jeb good-bye*. It had all happened so fast . . .

He stared, transfixed, while the Big Blue Marble on his screens shrank to the size of a real marble, and his eyes ached with longing.

When the Earth was no longer visible on any of the screens, he replaced it with the image of the sun. The sun showed its true form now, as the nearest star among the countless millions visible out here, where no atmosphere, and no atmospheric pollution, hid them from view.

No use crying over spilled milk, flyboy. He tried to remember that this journey to another world was probably their last chance at saving their own . . . that whether it really required him or not, this mission was important.

He glanced at the time elapsed: still thirteen hours to go until they reached Mercury's orbit . . . until he had even a single responsibility, or semi-meaningful duty to perform. He planted his elbow on the seat arm, resting his chin on his hand. His other hand began to drum a rhythm on his knee.

Maybe he'd take a nap. A long one . . . He leaned back, closing his eyes.

And all the while, Dr. Zachary Smith slept on, in the service bay on the lower level; blissfully unconscious . . . for now.

Don woke up again long before the thirteen hours had passed. He occupied himself with repeating systems checks and performing useless calibrations, wishing he'd at least thought to bring along a magazine, or his VR headset.

At last Mercury's choleric red face, now nearly the size of Earth's moon, lay centered in the wide viewport. Below it and to one side, a fraction of the sun's surface showed, blindingly bright even through the viewport's integral filters. Don kept his eyes fixed on the image in his monitors as he closed the blast shields over all the ship's ports, readying the *Jupiter* for its dive into the solar gravity well.

Now we get to the fun part. He grimaced. His sole responsibility in the upcoming maneuver was simply to lock the doors before he went to bed. He glanced over his shoulder at the last open cryo tube. *He wouldn't even be awake to see the real spectacle.*

He activated his headset. "Houston," he said, "diverting all spacecraft controls to the main computer." The CPU was the real commander of this ship. It would calculate the exact angle of their hyperbolic plunge through the sun's immensely powerful gravitational field. It would determine the precise timing and length of the engine burn that would keep the *Jupiter* from being swallowed by the sun's fusion furnace, and instead sling it back out into space. Using the momentum of their headlong "fall" to play crack-the-whip, they would boost their velocity to near lightspeed, cutting years from their voyage.

Once the real journey was under way, the computer would take care of everything: maintaining the *Jupiter*'s operating systems; tending to its frozen passengers (including him); making any course corrections; and finally waking them all up, on arrival at Alpha Prime.

The computer would do it all.

"Eight years of flight training," he muttered, flexing his restless hands. He slipped one of the three music CDs he'd managed to bring with him into the spare drive on the console, and cranked the volume up. Unstrapping from his seat, he walked to the center of the bridge and activated the navigational holograph. Images of colored light formed in midair above the instrument pedestal, showing *Jupiter Two* in its position near the sun, at the center of a slowly spinning graphic of the solar system.

"Navigational holographics on line," he said, into the mike on his headset; and, to himself, "*Fifty* combat missions." The points of light flitted eerily over his face and body as he moved among them. He highlighted the ship's trajectory past Mercury, around the sun in a U-shaped arc, and into space beyond. "Course confirmed for slingshot exit of the solar system," he reported dutifully.

He crossed the bridge toward the cryo tube that lay waiting for him. "Just so I can take the family camper on an interstellar picnic . . ." He climbed in and the preset controls activated. The monitored biopads of his suit closed him into their insensate embrace; he tried not to squirm. "Ten World Series," he said, raising his voice. "My nephews' high school and college graduations. A decade's worth of *Sports Illustrated* swimsuit editions! Lord *knows* how many wives—" He took a last look at the fully automated bridge; listened to his music playing. "Noah," he murmured, "ten years is a lifetime . . ." The final pad slid across his face, shielding his eyes.

"Sleep well, old friend." He heard Noah's voice, like a benediction.

"I never liked these freezing tubes," he murmured, his muscles tensing as the pod began to close. *Not even hearing about them* . . . "Bad dreams." *He'd never dreamed he'd ever have to—*

The cryo field engulfed him, and his brain whited out for the duration.

The last pod rose slowly into its chamber in the hull, joining the five already resting there, enshrouded in stillness and blue light. The ship flew on through the darkness toward its rendezvous with the sun, accompanied by music that no one heard.

Smith started awake from a nightmare into . . . a nightmare. Memory goaded him like an electric prod, and he scrambled up the lightless disposal chute into the robot bay. The bay's dim illumination seemed as bright as day to him now. Blinking, he focused on his throbbing hand; saw the impression of the overloaded communicator's circuits burned into his palm.

He looked right and left, still only half certain that he was not trapped in a horrible dream. He looked down at his watch, checking the time, and the feeling only grew stronger.

Stumbling toward a viewport, he hit the stud on the display panel below it. The blast shield opened.

He looked out on deep space.

Smith stared at the view for a long time, with the interior of his mind as empty as the night outside.

The computer console behind him abruptly came online, shocking him back into his senses in time to see something move on the other side of the room. Expecting to see a crew member, his mind struggled to comprehend the alien thing detaching itself from an alcove along the wall.

The robot. A huge industrial machine with two sets of arms, it looked like some monstrous gene-meld of man and beetle. It had been designed for construction work in space, but programmed to maintain *Jupiter Two* during its journey to Alpha Prime.

Surely it should not be doing anything yet.

Except that he had changed its programming.

"No—" he whispered. He tried to activate the burned-out programming module he had used last night. The keypad was as dead as he should have been.

"Disable program," he ordered aloud.

Oblivious, the robot used its skilled-work arms to finish disengaging from its mooring. It rolled forward into the bay on flexible tractor treads. *"Robinson family,"* it said. *"Destroy."* The flatness of its machine voice made his flesh crawl.

"Cease," he ordered, more loudly. "Desist!"

The robot rolled on by, never hesitating. *"All operating systems: Destroy."*

He realized where it was headed . . . to the bridge, on the upper level. He jerked a wrench from a tool bracket and ran after it. He didn't care if the Robinsons died. He didn't care if the entire world died. But if the robot got to the control room, *he* was a dead man—

As he caught up to it, the robot swung a massive

grappling arm at him without even looking back. It caught him in the chest, and hurled him aside like a fly. He slammed into the console that linked the service bay with the ship's main computer; its systems bleated and crackled as he slid down to the floor.

The robot rolled on, unconcerned, with only one command in its logic systems: "Jupiter Two: *Destroy*."

Roughly sixty million miles away, and currently on the night side of Earth, darkened screens flickered to life in the now peaceful Mission Control room. Annie, the lone technician on midnight watch, looked up in surprise from her guitar. She leaned forward, stared, and switched on her mike. "Somebody wake up the Chief," she said.

Chapter
Seven

The robot entered the *Jupiter*'s bridge and halted, as
the ship's central processing unit brought up the lights
and provided it with instant schematics for every piece
of equipment its sensors registered. It moved toward the
cryo sleep array, raw energy arcing between its extended
welding claws as it raised its arms.

The main computer, which controlled the robot's
every action, knew all about the humans held in suspended animation here: *those strange, organically based
computers; such fragile systems, so easily disrupted.* It
knew how to maintain them, how to repair them . . .
how to terminate them. Humans had programmed it,
and it knew its duty: *"Cryo sleep systems: Destroy."*

The robot released a burst of energy, blasting the cryo
sleep control console. Alarms sounded as the tubes
began to descend; electricity sparked across the sleeping
bodies.

The robot moved on, toward the navigation pedestal.
It stopped, facing the navigational holograph in the center of the bridge, observing the eerie beauty of the display. The air laced with lightning between its claws as
another charge began to build. The robot understood

the function and maintenance of these systems much more clearly. It understood what it must do. *"Navigational systems: Destroy."*

The Mission Control room lit up like a navigational display, as exhausted techies booted up their consoles to the flashing of alarms.

Noah strode into the room, looking much as he always did except for the expression on his face. He stood staring at the signs of disaster unfolding across one monitor after another. *What in hell—? What in hell . . . ?* "This mission's over!" he shouted. "Wake them up!"

His people were on it before he could finish the sentence. Annie looked up from her console, her face stricken. "No response, sir," she said.

Smith arrived on the bridge, his head bleeding from the robot's blow, just in time to see the robot fire on the navigational array. He cried out as the pedestal exploded and the holographic starmap blinked out of existence. More alarms began to sound as the ship's navigational systems went down, leaving it a rudderless boat, caught in the tidal drag of the sun's gravitational pull . . .

The robot moved on, toward the command center.

Smith stumbled to the cryotubes as he saw them swallowed in flames and smoke. "Wake up, damn you!" He worked frantically at the console, not even sure if he was speaking to the Robinsons or the ruins of the controls, "I can't stop this infernal contraption on my own!"

His eyes fell on a protected array that read EMER-GENCY DEACTIVATE. He smashed it open with his fist. Looking up, he saw the figures inside the erratically descending tubes begin to glow . . . all but one.

At the side of his vision lightning arced again between the robot's pincers. *"Command systems: Destroy."* The robot lifted its arms, taking aim.

More alarms sounded as the cryotubes began to open. The robot spun back on its treads. *"Robinson family: Destroy."*

As it rolled forward, Smith dove into the smoke and found a hole to crawl into.

John Robinson came suddenly, terribly, awake—pitched headlong out of the deepest dreams of nothing-ness by braying alarms, smoke, and explosions. He took one vertiginous step out of the cryotube and stopped, staring at the naked face of chaos worn by a berserk maintenance robot.

And then he threw himself out of the tube and rolled, drawing the robot's aim away from the cryo array, as his survival instincts were commandeered by the military training of his youth. "Maureen—" he shouted, driven by an instinct equally hard-wired. "The children!"

Maureen gaped for the length of a heartbeat, before the same unquestioning instinct set her moving. She dragged Penny and Will from their units, pulling them under cover behind a work station just as the robot's blast destroyed the place where they stood.

John wrenched a pistol from a wall mount. "Disengage safety," he gasped, swinging back around.

"*Voiceprint confirmed*," the gun said.

John fired. The laser burst struck the robot's head and set it reeling on its swivel.

The robot stabilized, and turned to face him. *No effect.*

John ducked behind a control pedestal as lightning lanced from its upraised claws. The concussive blast took out the pedestal in front of him and hurled him back against a wall; his gun went flying.

"Dad!" Will cried out, watching in anguish from his place beside his mother. If even a laser couldn't stop the robot— *But you don't fight fire with fire; you fight fire with water.* Will slammed his hand against the elevator call button on the support beside him; as it began to descend, he slipped under his mother's arm and bolted toward it.

"Will, wait!" Maureen dove after him, but he escaped her like a startled rabbit. Across the room the robot turned, tracking him with upraised arms.

Don West flung himself onto the machine's back as it fired; the blast went wide, and Will slid across the floor into the disappearing elevator. West clung to the robot's carapace, struggling to dislodge its power pack.

The robot sent a pulse of electricity through its metal shell, and West went flying. He hit the floor across the room like a rag doll, his cryo suit glowing with witchfire as its circuitry seared and fused.

The robot's platelike skull swiveled; it fixed the glaring red eye of its sensor array on the final spot where humans were still hiding. Its hulking, insectoid body wheeled on its treads in the smoking ruins; telltale lightning arced between its claws.

Maureen turned her back on it, shielding her daughter's body with her own. "Look away, baby," she whispered. She shut her own eyes, her body paralyzed with anticipation, waiting for the blast to strike her, *waiting—*

Nothing happened. Still nothing happened.

An eternity of heartbeats later she looked around again, her face clenched—

The robot stood motionless, its arms harmlessly at its sides. As she watched, its displays blinked from online to standby mode.

Across the room, Will stepped from the rising elevator with his hacking deck—the one that she had sworn more than once he would never see again—held triumphantly in his hands. "Robot," he said. "Return to your docking bay and power down."

"Command accepted," the robot said.

As Maureen watched in stunned disbelief, the robot headed obediently through the smoke toward the elevator. Her husband and Don West stirred, pushing themselves up to watch it pass.

Will grinned at her, with something gleaming in his eyes that could have been, *Told you, Mom* . . .

A note of hysterical laughter escaped her; she laughed

again, her eyes filling with pride and love as she looked back at him. *Like father, like son* ...

"If the family won't come to the science fair," Will said, gazing around the room in satisfaction, "bring the science fair to the family."

"Show off," Penny murmured, as she edged out from behind her mother. But a reluctant smile of genuine admiration pulled up the corners of her mouth.

"Where's Judy—?" Maureen said suddenly. She started back through the miasma of smoke and sparking circuitry toward the cryo array.

John reached down, offering his hand to Don West, who was struggling to get to his feet. "Next picnic, no robots," West muttered thickly, shaking himself out. He pushed away from John's support with a nod, coughing as he headed through the smoke toward the helm.

The bridge had become a scene out of Dante's *Inferno*: fire and smoke and twisted ruins everywhere. The navigation array was gone from the air, its pedestal destroyed.

My God ... John's gaze went to the viewport, shuttered by blast shields. He ran to his seat at the com and began to work.

Next to him, Penny sat down at another intact console, and began trying to bring up the fire control systems. FIRE SYSTEMS flashed on her displays—and then the screen suddenly went dark. The console died in a shower of electrical sparks. Penny's hands made fists as she jerked away from the keyboard. "I want to go home now..." she said, her voice caught somewhere between joking and tears. She massaged her stinging hands, and went back to work.

"No course data," John called out to West. "System shorts everywhere." He hit a stud on his seat arm. The chair ascended, taking him up to the overhead access panel. He pried it open and went to work on the circuitry inside.

Below him, Penny got the fire control systems stabilized. Extinguishers activated around the room, smothering blazes with chemical foam.

"I can't open her blast shields," Don reported. "I'll try remote ops."

He started across the room through the pall of smoke. As he passed Will's work station, someone groaned. He ducked down into the reeking smoke, groping on the floor until he found what felt like a human body, and dragged it upright. "*Smith?*" he said in disbelief. "What the hell—"

Smith began to struggle, shouting, "Get back! Leave me alone!" Don fended off the incoherent blows, holding on to the other man until Smith's mind cleared.

"Major West," Smith gasped, with actual recognition. "Thank God it's you! I . . . I was making a last-minute check . . . someone hit me from behind." He raised his hand to his head, wincing. Don saw the smear of drying blood on the side of his face.

And then his surprise and concern immolated. He reached out, grabbing Smith's upraised hand.

Seared into Smith's palm was the perfect image of a reprogramming module . . . but not one he had ever used. "Sedition technology," Don said hoarsely. "You're a goddamned spy!" Before the words were even out of his mouth, their full implication hit him. "*You* did this—"

He slammed Smith against the wall with all his strength, then dragged him toward the airlock. He hit the access button with his fist, and the airlock's inner hatch swung open.

"Stop," Smith gasped in disbelief. "What are you doing?"

"Throwing out the trash." Don shoved him backward, trying to force his rigid body through the hatchway.

"Help, somebody! Please—" Maureen Robinson's desperate voice barely penetrated his rage.

Don looked over his shoulder, holding Smith pinned. He saw Maureen standing by the cryo console, only realizing then that one of the units had never opened. Its cryofield sparked on and off; the sight made his stomach turn. *Whose—? Judy's.*

"Her thawing engine is broken!" Maureen said. "I can't get her out. She's dying—" Her eyes searched the room for someone who knew cryo technology.

He didn't. Who did? . . . Only Judy.

Smith wrenched a hand free and drove it upward, the palm catching Don under the chin. Don staggered; came back at him, as fury anesthetized the pain of the blow.

"Touch me and the girl dies—" Smith said, his eyes burning.

Don froze, inches away from breaking Smith's neck like a stick.

"Your mission physican is indisposed," Smith murmured, glancing at the cryo array. Don thought he actually heard an edge of mockery in the words, as if Smith's brain was something alien, inhabiting the man's cringing body. "I can save her life," Smith said. "But only if you spare mine."

You psychopathic bastard. Don tightened his grip. "I don't deal with dead men," he said. He had never meant anything so completely in his life.

"Kill me, kill the girl," Smith gasped. "How much is your revenge worth? . . . Major?" Smith looked into Don's eyes; a faint smile pulled at his lips. "I will, of course, need your word as an officer that you will let me live."

Don hesitated, barely able to control his trembling hands. Then, finally, he let Smith go. "Help her."

He backed off, letting Smith pass. He watched the doctor cross the room, making certain Smith went directly to the cryo console.

Abruptly, the command console where John Robinson was working squawked to life. ". . . is Mission Control. Do you read? *Jupiter Two*, this is—"

Don glanced away from Smith, up at Robinson. "Power reserves online," Robinson called down from the access, oblivious to what was happening below. "Blast shields . . . got it!"

Don started toward the viewport as the blast shields began to open. Agonizing brightness struck him in the eyes. The sun, enormous and inescapable, filled his entire vision.

"Uh-oh . . ." he whispered, as words failed him.

The face of Noah Freeman appeared on his displays. "You're way off course!" Noah said. "We show you in the sun's gravitational pull."

Don looked away from the sun's face to Noah's. He grimaced. "Is *that* what that big round ball is—?" *Mission Control had a real gift for understatement.*

Back on Earth, Noah looked up at his own screens, seeing what Don saw now. Noah's lips moved, off-mike; Don realized he was swearing.

"Noah," he said, as John's chair descended beside him, "how come we never talk when things are going well?"

"We count seven minutes before your outer hull begins to melt," Noah said, as calmly and to-the-point as if he hadn't just taken the same psychological hit in the gut.

Easy for him to stay cool, damn him. Don settled into the pilot's chair. *He's sixty million miles away.*

Sitting in the ruins of the bridge, staring down the throat of the sun, he realized at last why they had wanted a real pilot for this mission...

"I'm going to try for the Mercury Mines," he said, his hands already at work on the console's keyboard.

Chapter
Eight

Across the bridge Maureen Robinson worked with Smith, following his terse instructions to the letter as they tried to save her daughter from the damaged cryotube. She observed his obvious skill and expertise; respecting them, as she had during all the months the family had been preparing for this mission. She glanced up occasionally to see John and Don West working like men obsessed at the com; she saw the sun, bloated and violently yellow, filling the viewport. She felt absolutely nothing, beyond her overwhelming need to save Judy's life.

"I will need Dr. Robinson's portable gurney," Smith said abruptly. "I believe it is stored in—"

"I'm on it!" Penny left her side, running toward the elevator, before Maureen fully realized what the words meant: *Judy was almost free from the tube*. A vast rush of relief hit her. *The first, hardest part was nearly over*.

And with that, her insulating shield of control shattered, and all the emotion she had held in check came pouring through.

She looked back at Smith with a kind of disbelief, feeling as if she had never seen him before—knowing she had *never* seen the real man, in all the time they had worked together. "We *trusted* you," she said, hearing the outrage in her voice. "You tried to kill my family . . ."

Smith lifted an eyebrow, as if she had accused him of having bad manners. "Existence offers us nothing, if not the opportunity for an endless series of betrayals."

She stared at him, wondering if he had gone mad, or she had.

He looked at her; his gaze was clear and cold. "There is a world behind the world, Professor Robinson," he said gently, as if he were speaking to a child. "Lie once, cheat twice, and everything becomes clear . . . Do not mistake my deception for a character flaw. It is a philosophical choice, a profound understanding of the universe." His mouth quirked. "It is a way of life."

"You're a monster," she said, with soft fury.

"Perhaps." Smith shrugged. "But I am also the only one who can save your daughter's life." He nodded as Penny stepped out of the elevator, towing the floating gurney.

"All right, Penny precious," he said, in the tone of voice Maureen had always heard as kindly, before now. Now it only sounded condescending, as if he was mocking them all. "I need you to short the power, on my command."

"Does he have to call me '*precious*'?" Penny said, her mouth pulling down. She had never liked Smith. Maureen had always told herself it was just Penny's cynical streak. But maybe Penny had been the best judge of human nature all along.

"Professor, you will assist me in lowering the body," Smith directed, handing Penny a wrench without even glancing at her. As they moved into position, he looked back at her again, finally, and smiled. "Penny, *precious*... Now."

Penny looked at her mother, defiance and fury reddening her face. Maureen nodded.

Penny swung the wrench, slamming it against the power unit as if she wished it was Smith's skull. The cryo field deactivated in a flash of light. The tube swung open, and the lifesigns monitor beside Judy flat-lined with a desolate whine.

"She's not breathing!" Maureen caught her daughter's limp body, and they lowered her onto the gurney.

"Sickbay," Smith snapped, suddenly the doctor Maureen remembered again. "Move!"

Together they pushed the gurney out through the blast doors to the waiting elevator.

The doors closed and the elevator began to descend. They barely noticed the lurch as the entire ship shuddered, struggling to break free of the sun's grasp.

Don swore, as his final attempt to boost the ship free of the sun's gravitational drag failed. "The sun won't let us go," he said into the mike. "Noah, I need options—"

"Major West," Noah said at last, his voice still unnervingly professional, "we are unable to provide contingencies."

Don looked at the displays.

As Noah registered his expression, he murmured, "I'm sorry, Don . . ."

"We've got to divert all power to the engines," Robinson

said, still working at his controls. "Rerouting Life Sciences."

Don said nothing, as the nonessential Life Sciences systems went offline. Robinson might be a genius, but a physicist's view of the universe was like a VR game, where anything could happen. Don lived in the real universe, where a good pilot knew what wasn't possible . . .

But that didn't mean he'd give up trying for a miracle.

The drive core indicator on his panel showed a power increase. "Robotics," Robinson said, and as he shut it down, the engine capacity jumped again.

"Medical—"

As Robinson put through one more power shunt, the damaged system crashed. Electricity arced across consoles, shorting more of them out; SHUNT ERROR flashed on his monitor, WARNING: MEDICAL SYSTEMS CRASH. "No!" Robinson gasped, starting up out of his seat. "*Judy—*"

"No cardiopulmonary or respiratory functions," Smith said.

Maureen stared at the scanners above the diagnostic table where Judy lay. A holoschematic of her body shimmered in the air, above her frighteningly still real one. Her heart was highlighted in red.

Smith activated the cardiac stimulus program. "Clear," he said.

Judy's body jerked on the table; the holographic heart beat once, and was still.

"Again," Smith said sharply. "Clear."

Lights flickered on the bio console, and the holograph winked out.

Maureen sucked in a breath. "We're losing her!"

Smith's eyes raked the room, searching for any equipment that hadn't gone down. There was none. He leaned over Judy's body and began manual CPR, pressing down on her sternum, forcing her heart to beat by sheer physical pressure. "Come on, child," he murmured. "*Fight*. Put a little heart in it!" When Judy still did not respond, he stepped back and with his fist began precise, staccato blows to her chest.

Maureen watched him, white-knuckled. Smith almost seemed human again, caught up in the work of a physician—as if it really mattered to him whether he saved her daughter's life; as if the person she had believed he was still existed, somewhere inside him.

But then she realized what he was saying, under his breath, as he jarred Judy's recalcitrant heart again and again: "The life . . . I save . . . may be . . . my own . . ."

He stopped suddenly, pressing his ear to Judy's chest. He took her pulse. He smiled.

Maureen pushed past him. "Judy? *Baby*—?"

Judy's eyes flickered open; somehow, she managed a weak smile. "You should try to look less worried," she whispered faintly. "It has a tendency to spook the patients."

Maureen looked up at Smith, suddenly not caring whether he was the most hideous monster ever to walk the Earth. "Thank you," she said, from the bottom of her heart.

"I hope I have proven the well-being of your family is of great import to me," Smith said, smiling back at her. "You are a good woman, Professor Robinson, anyone can see that. Perhaps, if you convinced your husband to trust me . . ." His eyes were like stones.

Maureen jerked a medical laser free from its wall bracket. She pinpointed his forehead, her expression even colder than his. "Stabilize her, Smith. Because you only breathe as long as she does."

"Heat seal breach in forty seconds," the computer said.

The console showed engine capacity at one hundred and fifty percent. "That's all the power we've got," Robinson said.

Don nodded. "I'm putting the pedal to the metal. Here goes." He engaged the main thrusters. Vibration shook the ship like a dog with a chew toy, as he bet all the power they had against the law of gravity, in a last-ditch wager to win the *Jupiter's* freedom.

And lost.

"She can't break free!" Don cut the engines, before the riptide of counterstresses tore the ship apart. "She doesn't have enough thrust." He shook his head, staring at the displays as the *Jupiter* resumed its long fall toward the surface of the sun.

"There's got to be some way to get through this—!" Robinson said, his eyes raking the control panels.

Don wondered whether Robinson was addressing him, or God. Because the only thing that would save them now was a real miracle . . .

Don turned in his seat to stare at John. "That's it."

"What's it?" Robinson asked, looking around; but Don had already ascended his chair toward the hyperdrive initiator.

"If we can't go around the sun," Don shouted, "we have to go through it! Using your hyperdrive—"

"If we engage the hyperdrive without a gate, we could be thrown anywhere in the galaxy!" Robinson got to his feet, shaking his head.

"Anywhere but here," Don said.

Robinson stared at him. And then he spun back to the console, thumbing a panel open. He took out two keys, tossed one up to Don. Inserting his key on the console, he said, "On my mark."

Don inserted his own key into the initiator console.

"Three–two–one—" Robinson recited, "initiate."

They turned the keys.

The images of Mission Control on the displays below dissolved into static. Don heard a barely audible voice saying, "We're getting resident radiation distortions from the spacecraft. She must be breaking up." Heard Noah demanding, "...me see those numbers, Annie—"

And the last thing he heard, before they lost all contact, was Noah Freeman's oddly elated voice saying, "*Son of a bitch.*"

Don put the displays on exterior view: the image showed the *Jupiter*'s saucer-form hull glowing like a forge, sweating droplets of alloy that vanished toward the billowing mountains of superheated gas below them.

"*Warning*," the computer said. "*Heat shield breach.*"

But now he *was* living in a physicists' universe . . . As he watched, the extending hyperdrive segments along the ship's perimeter flared with energy, and a shimmering force field enfolded the ship. The attenuators charged, and the ship seemed to elongate as it began its shift into another dimension. The sun's flaming face grew strangely distorted as the hyperdrive warped space around them.

"Hyperdrive is at one hundred percent," Robinson said. "Major, you have the com."

Facing the hungry sun Don grinned, as much an act of defiance as of belief. "Let's see what this baby can do . . ." He engaged the hyperdrive.

"Dad—" Will Robinson's voice said, behind them.

From the corner of his eye, Don saw Robinson leap from his seat and start across the bridge to his son. He opened his mouth to—

Before he could call out the warning, everything changed.

Robinson and his son were flung across the room by suddenly shifting gravity, as an invisible wave of transforming energy broke over them all. Belowdecks, it caught Maureen and Penny, and Smith wrapping Judy in thermal blankets; swept them all aside.

As it swept Don from his seat, the hull began to disappear, and around him sections of the ship winked randomly out of existence.

The same wave passed through all their minds at once, stopping thought as the impossible became reality; their bodies froze in midflight, along with time itself, as the universe swallowed its tail . . . and what happened after that was beyond all comprehension.

In Mission Control, the graphic representation of the *Jupiter* began to flicker, merging into the graphic of the sun. Noah stared at the screen as Annie said, "We can't keep a fix on her, sir."

Noah released the breath he had been holding uselessly, and murmured, "Godspeed . . ."

The first leaping tongue of atomic flame kissed the *Jupiter Two*'s elongated hull; but her shimmering, intangible form had already passed beyond its reach.

The ship fell through the sun, untouched, untouchable, her translucent disk drawn wire-thin, before she vanished from known space in a sudden flare of light.

Chapter Nine

The nameless world rolled through the void, its journey around distant binary suns undisturbed for eons.

Until now. High above its ruddy surface a wormhole opened in space, and a ship fell through into the starry void. The name of the ship was the *Jupiter Two*.

The nameless world would never be the same.

Maureen Robinson kneeled on the floor beside Penny, making sure her daughter was really all right, and not just too dazed to tell her what was wrong. The mind-twisting Something that had seized them all had left no visible aftereffects, at least down here. Smith seemed to have been struck speechless; but in her opinion, that was hardly a problem. She glanced up, reassuring herself that he was still standing sullenly, arms folded, in the same spot across the room.

She got to her feet, thinking of John and Will . . . and looked up in relief as John entered the room.

John stopped in the doorway, seeing his wife and Penny and Smith—and an empty gurney. "Judy?" he asked. "Where's Judy?"

As if on cue, his eldest child stepped through a doorway at the far side of the room. Still in the process of fastening her coveralls, she said, "Boy, either I cut down on the coffee or sew in a flap. It's hell getting in and out of that thing." She smiled as his incredulous gaze met hers.

"Are you—" John began.

"Vitals are normal," she said, still maddeningly nonchalant. "Pulse and respiration seem to be—"

"Baby, are you *okay*—?" he demanded, crossing the room. She might be a grown woman and a doctor, she might even be better at being him than *he* was; but she was still, would always be, his firstborn child.

Judy broke off, her expression changing as if she only now realized that he was upset. "I'm *fine*, Daddy," she said gently, "really."

God, he thought, *am I that much of a human cypher?* He held her close, overwhelmed by the emotions filling him, now that his fear of losing her was gone.

Someone made a small, disgusted noise behind him. "Will every little problem be an excuse for familial sentiment?" Smith asked sourly.

John turned away from his daughter to face Smith, and the emotion overwhelming him was suddenly pure rage. "How much, Smith!" he shouted into the other man's face. "What was the price tag you put on our future—?" not even sure whether he meant the world's future or only his family's.

Smith retreated through the doorway into the medical lab, raising his fists as if John's words had been blows. John felt his own hands tighten into fists, aching to lash out. He took a step forward—

Just as Will entered the room.

His clenched fists fell open, and dropped to his sides. Looking at Will, he shook his head.

Smith stared at him, uncomprehending. And then he lowered his hands. "You can't do it, can you?" he murmured. "You *can't* kill me." His eyes came alive: *I know you* . . . they said. His mouth twisted with amusement and disgust. "Ah, the virtue of high-minded ideals. You can't kill the man, without becoming a monster . . ."

John held Smith's gaze through an agonizing length of silence; until he realized that nothing he could possibly say to this man would have any more effect than saying nothing at all. He turned his back on Smith then, his own mouth a knife slash of frustration.

"Coward," Smith said, and John heard the smile in it.

John spun back, the flat of his hand slamming into the control stud on the wall beside him as if it was Smith's face. The door of the medical lab into which Smith had retreated dropped like a guillotine's blade, sealing him inside.

John stepped away from the door, breathing hard, his muscles knotted as if he had actually been in a fight. Will stared up at him, looking puzzled and a little frightened. John tried to force his face back into something like a normal expression.

"What happened, John?" Maureen came to his side, and he knew from the look on her face that the question had nothing to do with Smith. She put a hand on his arm; he felt her fingers tighten like steel bands. "Where are we?"

He took a deep breath.

❖   ❖   ❖

Don had just finished taking the hyperdrive offline and reinitiating the ship's main systems when the Robinsons reentered the bridge. He watched about half the monitors in the room come back to life, and then let his chair descend. "I've bypassed most of the damaged systems," he said. "We'll have to repair the rest manually."

He saw Judy standing with her parents; surprised to see her up and around, more surprised by the enormous sense of relief that filled him. "You had me worried, Doc. Nice to see you thawed."

Judy smiled and shrugged, as if she regarded a near-death experience as No Big Deal. "You have the most puzzling definition of a smooth ride . . ."

Don grinned briefly, ruefully, in acknowledgment. *Too bad she became a doctor,* he thought. *She would have made a hell of a pilot.*

He crossed the room to the navigation pedestal and brought its rebooted system online. A holograph of the *Jupiter Two* appeared above its surface. "Computer, map our current location."

The holo display shimmered, and when it cleared again, the area around the *Jupiter* was filled with a holographic representation of a solar system he had definitely never seen before. "*Searching for recognizable stellar configurations,*" the computer said tonelessly. There were none. They all watched, riveted by the sight as the starfield continued to expand, while the image of the *Jupiter* shrank until it was no longer identifiable within the swarming mass of lights.

"This data base has starmaps of the entire known galaxy," John Robinson said finally, very quietly.

"I don't recognize a single system." Don shrugged, shaking his head.

"We're lost, aren't we?" Penny Robinson asked. Her voice sounded very small and far away, as if it reached him from somewhere beyond this artificial construct of the stars they knew . . . somewhere in the endless reaches of uncharted space.

He didn't answer. He didn't need to.

Chapter Ten

Judy slowly removed another piece of Don West's fused cryo suit from his naked back, feeling her eyes take a highly unprofessional interest in his muscles. *God, he has a nice body* ... She gave herself a mental kick, grateful that she was standing behind him. *What is wrong with me—?*

She had known he had a nice body from the first moment she saw him. And a face to match, somehow sweet and funny and heart-stoppingly handsome all at once; with blue, blue eyes ... nice hair, incredibly kissable lips. She hadn't been able to take her eyes off him ... until he'd opened his mouth.

And then he'd become just another flyboy: a walking ego, who let his little head do all the thinking for his big head. She'd met way too many of those to let this one get near her, let alone get under her skin.

She'd seen a lot of men—a lot of them naked, after she'd decided to become a doctor. It wasn't like she'd been a nun in those days, either. But since she had begun working on this mission . . . realized that the future of the entire planet could rest on its success . . . she'd barely noticed whether the people she worked with were male or female. How could she think about herself, when that was so much more important?

So why did she still want to run her hands over Don West's shoulders, feel those strong, well-muscled arms slide around her back . . . *Stop it!* She pried lose another piece of his suit.

So she'd nearly died a couple of hours ago. So what—?

If only he could keep his mouth shut . . .

Don stood as still as possible in the center of sickbay while Judy finished freeing him from his cryo suit. He'd been in crisis mode until now, running on adrenaline, feeling no pain. But as soon as he'd had time to draw a calm breath, he'd realized that he had to get out of this thing—and he couldn't. He felt bruised and singed all over from the electrical charge that damned robot had sent through the suit. He was lucky nothing worse had happened; hell, he was lucky he was alive. They all were.

He glanced again at the medical lab where John Robinson had imprisoned Smith: just one more specimen trapped in a jar. Smith was beating his fists on the shatterproof window again, shouting something inaudibly. Judy Robinson went calmly about her business, never even acknowledging Smith's presence; as if having a homicidal lunatic locked in her closet was No Big Deal either. Don met the malevolent fury in Smith's eyes, and grinned nastily.

"Hold still," Judy murmured.

"I'm trying to," he protested, scratching his suit-covered shoulder fruitlessly. "Can't you hurry it up?" By now nagging itches and his stressed-out nerves were beginning to plague every centimeter of his body that didn't already hurt . . . not to mention the fact that he really, *really* needed to take a leak.

Judy made a small, sympathetic noise, and touched his still-armored shoulder. "The cryo suit absorbed most of the robot's electrical charge," she said. "You're lucky this isn't your hide . . ."

He twisted around to look at her. "Doctor, is that concern I detect in your voice?" he asked hopefully.

Judy ripped the recalcitrant piece of seared suit from his shoulder like a swath of adhesive.

"*Ouch,*" Don protested. "Great bedside manner."

Judy looked up at him, and what he saw in her eyes then made his heart jump. Her gaze dropped away to the scar on his upper arm. "What's this?" she asked, running her fingers lightly down it. "A battle scar?"

Goose bumps started on his flesh at her touch, spreading down his arm. He hoped she didn't notice. "Kind of," he said, smiling. "Was a tattoo. Ex-girlfriend. I had it removed."

Judy looked back him. She raised an eyebrow. "Wouldn't it be easier just to use a Magic Marker?"

Another direct hit. Every time he thought he had her in his sights, she jagged. *This one was an ace.* He shaped his grimace into a grin. "That's me . . ." he said. "A girl in every port."

Judy stared at him for a long moment, as if she'd heard how hollow that sounded; just like he had. "So, no family,

Major?" she asked, turning back to her work. She wasn't baiting him now; he had no clue where her thoughts were. "Nothing to tie you down? Nothing to miss . . . ?" She looked up at his face, and away again. She peeled another piece of suit off him, carefully this time.

He didn't know how to answer her, because he didn't know what kind of answer she expected from him. So he told her the truth. "I've never been the fit-in-and-play-nice type. After a while, the part of me folks want to see most is my back, going out the door."

He remembered his parents suddenly; remembered the slam of the broken screen door, the blistered paint peeling from the side of the house and how the red dust had clung to his pants legs, as he walked away . . . He looked down, even though she was no longer looking at him.

"I guess you think that's romantic," Judy murmured, peeling away the last of the ruined cryo suit from his chest.

He looked back at her. "No," he said. "No, I don't."

She met his stare, her green eyes targeting his soul.

"How about you, Doc?" He fired a personal question at her, before she could nail him. "Is there some lucky little nerd you left behind?"

He'd almost blown it; let her slip through his defenses. He told himself it was just that way too much had happened to him, way too fast, these past few days. But something eeled through the depths of his brain, reminding him that now he was trapped with these people, on this ship, indefinitely . . .

Somehow that was worse than being alone. *We're not lost! I can find the way home; I'm the best there is—*

"I have spent the last three years preparing for this mission," Judy said, folding her arms. Her eyes were cold as he looked back at her, letting him know his evasive maneuver had worked all too well. "We are trying to save the planet here, Major. I haven't had time for *fun.*"

Inside the words he heard depths of frustration and loss he didn't want to feel . . . feelings she didn't even seem to be aware of.

He shrugged on the neatly folded gray T-shirt she had laid out for him. The cloth felt like sandpaper against his skin . . . or maybe a hair shirt.

He started for the door; stopped, midway across the room. He looked back at her where she stood, her body still clenched and unforgiving. Two hours ago she'd almost died, because of this mission . . . "If there's no time for fun, Doc," he asked gently, half smiling, "then what are we saving the planet for?"

She stared at him, motionless and silent. She watched him all the way across the room and out the door.

Will Robinson stood on tiptoe in the robot bay, trying to dislodge a giant bubble diode from the wall. He glanced around in surprise as Penny's arms suddenly reached in beside his own, and helped him pull the component free.

"Thanks." Will smiled and sat down, settling the diode carefully in his lap. He looked up at her, making a rueful face. "I hate being little."

Penny held out her cam/watch in response. "I think it broke."

Will took it from her and looked it over, suddenly not feeling so small and useless; instead feeling the sense of confidence and competence that he only had when he looked at something mechanical. He almost *knew*, just by looking at it, how it should work; where the malfunction was, if it didn't. He picked a tool out of his kit and began to tinker with the camcorder.

"Why aren't you up on deck with Mom and Dad?" Penny asked.

He glanced up. "Have you *met* our parents?" he said sullenly.

Penny made a prune face. "Good point." She sighed, looking at the wall.

Will hit the camcorder's playback button, and grinned as it began to speak, in Penny's voice. "...Popcorn. Orchids. Waves. Billy. Kissing..."

Penny snatched it out of his hands and shut it off, her face reddening. "It's a list," she said, to his curious stare. "Of everything we left behind." All at once there were tears in her eyes. She refused to let them fall, fixing him with a red-rimmed stare. "Never love anything, kiddo," she said angrily. "Because you just end up losing it!" She turned on her heel and strode out of the room.

Will watched her go, silently.

Maureen and John Robinson worked together at the Life Sciences console on the bridge, trying to restore as much of the life support system as they could salvage. Maureen watched her husband out of the corner of her eye, occasionally glancing over to give him input on the job he was doing as she concentrated on her own work. A small back corner of her thoughts drifted to the uniqueness of having her chronically preoccupied husband in a place where he actually had to listen to what she was saying.

Not that anyone wouldn't be preoccupied, under these circumstances . . .

"What was I thinking," he muttered, "dragging my family out into space?"

"What could we do, John?" she said, rerouting a segment of circuitry. "Leave them on Earth? Rob them of their parents, miss their growing up?"

He didn't answer, rummaging among the ruined components for something he could work with. "Smith can still hurt us," he said after a moment, and she realized that he hadn't really required an answer; his worries had simply gone on in silence. "Maybe I shouldn't let him live. . . . But—"

"But," she finished his thought, splicing wires, "'how can we bring civilization to the stars if we can't remain civilized' . . . right, Professor?" She knew he would recognize the words. They were his own; he repeated them every time he watched the news report.

John raised his head from the entrails of the console to give her an annoyed look. "Have you ever noticed you take the opposite position on whatever I say?"

"Of course I do," she said calmly, surprised that *he* had noticed. "We're married."

"What the hell—?" John exclaimed.

She looked back at him in genuine surprise, and then concern as she saw where he was looking now. She followed his gaze to the viewscreens across the room.

The uncharted planet in the center of the screens had begun to glow. As she watched, some sort of energy field flowed outward from its surface, distorting its image. The star-pricked blackness of space seemed to sear away around the edges of the distortion, leaving a glowing portal.

Beyond the portal, a long gleaming spindle of starship caught the light of this system's binary suns.

Across the bridge Don West echoed, "What the hell?"

Don pulled his gaze away from the anomaly that had seared a fire-ringed hole in space ahead of them, and turned in his seat to look at his mismatched crew. *His crew.* It was hard even to think of that word when he looked at them. But the entire Robinson family was here on the bridge with him, each of them working competently at an assigned station as they tried to get some kind of fix on what was out there. He had to admit, reluctantly, that there was no deadwood along on this family picnic.

"It appears to be some kind of rend in space," John Robinson reported.

"Where does it lead?" his wife asked.

"A reasonable question," Don murmured. He turned back to the console and engaged the thrusters.

"Major, wait—" Robinson said.

Don punched in the coordinates and sent the *Jupiter* into the glowing gap. "I'll wait later." He felt his pulse pick up as the gigantic silver ship loomed in their viewport.

"Pull back!" Robinson said sharply, crossing the room toward him. "That's an order—"

"Let there be light," Don said, as if he hadn't heard. He turned on the *Jupiter*'s forward searchlights. And gaped.

So did Robinson, standing beside him now.

"If this is all a dream," Don said plaintively, "why can't there be more girls?"

Caught in their spotlight beams, the hull of the unknown spindle-form ship stood out in gleaming detail, pied with what appeared to be scabs of metal plates. On its side was the designation PROTEUS. And beneath that, the same logo he wore on his uniform sleeve: ASOMAC.

"She's one of ours, all right," he said finally. "But I've never seen a ship like that." *God, it was enormous . . . it was beautiful. But how—?*

"No response to hails," Judy said.

"I'm getting inconsistent life signs," Maureen Robinson said, "but they may be sensor ghosts."

"Her computer could still be up." John worked at the copilots' console, his objections forgotten. "I'll try standard docking codes."

Ahead of them a docking ring on the ship's immense side came to life; lights illuminated the aperture that gave access to the ship's airlock as it rotated open.

Don guided the *Jupiter* toward it, passing a smaller secondary ring. Moored there already was another, far smaller craft; its sinuous, anthropomorphic lines were not even vaguely like anything he'd ever seen. "That's not one of ours."

"Boys," Maureen said, "that's not even *human*."

Chapter
Eleven

Walking the corridors of the lower deck, Don found Penny Robinson at work repairing a monitor as she emoted into the cam/watch on her wrist: "As a part of her enslavement, the Brave Space Captive, Penny Robinson, is forced to utilize her skills—" She broke off as she heard footsteps, and turned abruptly toward him. "Identify yourself, soldier," she said, hiding her embarrassment behind a halfhearted scowl.

He came to attention smartly. "West, Major, United Global Space Force, requesting permission to see the prisoner."

The muffled sound of something smashing into a wall punctuated his words. *This was the place where they'd locked Smith up, all right.*

Penny stepped aside, poker-faced. "Proceed, Major West."

Don smiled, and threw in a wink as he moved past her to the door. He was glad the kids were doing okay. Behind him he heard her mutter, "Ouch. Could he be *any* cuter? I don't think so . . ."

"Breathe, Penny, *breathe*," her little brother said, as he passed her in the hall.

Don's smile faded as he entered Smith's cell. The room's interior had been completely trashed; it looked like the robot had been in here. He was surprised Smith had the strength to throw a tantrum that big.

Smith sat in a chair, looking indignant, as if all the destruction had been done by poltergeists. "These quarters are totally unacceptable," he said.

Don ignored him, tossing the bundled fieldsuit he carried onto the cushions beside Smith. "We're going to check out the probe ship. Maybe we can figure out how they got here. And how to get home."

Smith settled himself more deeply in his seat. "*Ta-ta.* Have a wonderful trip." He bent his head at the door.

"You're coming with us," Don said, feeling Smith's sarcasm peel his nerves like fingernails on a blackboard.

Smith laughed once. "Out of the question," he said. "I'm a doctor, not a space explorer."

Don crossed the room in two strides, caught Smith by the front of his coveralls, and dragged him up out of his seat. "What *you* are is a murdering saboteur," he said furiously, "and I am *not* leaving you on this ship so you can do more harm than you've already caused!"

Smith pulled back, his jaw set. "I absolutely refuse—"

Don jerked him closer. "Give me an excuse to kill you. *Please,*" he whispered. He let go, holding Smith with his gaze until he was absolutely sure Smith believed he meant every word.

Smith smoothed his rumpled clothing. He smiled, as if they had been discussing the weather, and picked up the fieldsuit. "Black always was my color," he said, looking up again. His smile widened like a stain.

* * *

John entered the robot bay and took a plasma rifle out of the weapons locker. "Deactivate safety," he said.

"*Voiceprint confirmed*," the gun's microprocesser answered. "*Rifle is armed.*" A small light blinked from red to green.

"Crush."

John spun around with the rifle ready in his hands. His heart lurched as he saw the robot come through the doorway, waving its arms like a berserker.

"*Crush! Kill! Destroy!*" the robot blared.

John raised the gun, taking dead aim at the machine's control nexus. He almost fired, blasting it apart—would have, if the conditioning that had made him an expert marksman had not been so complete; if his father had not been so good, at everything.

He hesitated the extra fraction of a second, reconfirming his target—and saw the robot roll to a stop. Saw Will step out from behind it, hacker's deck in hand.

John lowered the rifle as if it suddenly weighed a ton. He stared at his son in disbelief. Will pulled a tiny microphone from his deck, and lifted it to his lips.

"Crush. Kill. Destroy," Will said.

"*Crush! Kill! Destroy!*" the robot echoed.

Will leaned familiarly on its humanoid carapace, and began to point out jury-rigged modifications. "I hacked into his CPU, bypassed his main operating system and accessed his subroutines." He looked up into his father's eyes. "He's basically running on remote control." *I saved all your lives, and you didn't even thank me!* Look *at what I did! Look at* me, *Dad—!* Will held his gaze, until John was the one who abruptly looked away.

"Will . . ." John began, trying to find a smile, "I know I haven't—"

Don West entered the room then, and said, "Professor, we're ready."

John glanced at West and frowned, before he looked back at his son. *I know you need me . . . But I have to remember the big picture . . . I have to protect you, and keep our family alive. That's what being a parent means.* Will stared at him with silent resignation. "We'll talk later, son," he said wearily.

He walked past Will and the robot, shouldering his gun as he went out of the room with West.

Will watched in silence as his father left him behind, again.

Why couldn't *he* be big enough to use a gun and go with his father like Don West, facing the same dangers, protecting *him* . . . doing something that would make Dad need him enough that he'd never leave him behind again. *He hated feeling small, and helpless, and useless—* He bit his lip.

He glanced at the robot, at its enormous, solid strength hovering protectively at his side. He turned, staring at it a moment longer. And then he input a command on his deck.

"Take care of my dad, okay, Robot?"

The robot rolled obediently out the door, following his father and West.

His voice still sounded very small in the vast, echoing space of this room. *He hated being small, and useless.* But now that he had the robot, he'd never have to be small and useless again.

Chapter Twelve

A long, dark corridor lay waiting for them as the *Proteus*'s airlock cycled open. Don activated the helmet light on his environmental suit; glanced back over his shoulder at the *Jupiter*'s airlock hatch before he took the first step into the unknown. Judy followed on his heels, with Smith behind her. John Robinson brought up the rear, to make sure Smith didn't cut and run.

And behind them all, incongruously, came the robot that was responsible for their being in this mess.

He shook his head. *No* . . . It *hadn't been responsible*. It *was just a machine*. Smith had reprogrammed it, that was all. The robot followed their orders now, and it gave them access to the *Jupiter*'s analytical systems as they explored.

"Oxygen levels are normal," he heard Judy say through his helmet speakers, as the airlock resealed behind them. "Microbe scans are negative. Clear."

He raised a gauntleted hand, retracting his helmet into the yoke of his equipment harness, as the others did the same.

Judy took a deep breath as they started on again. "The air is stale," she said. "Old."

"That's the smell of ghosts . . ." Smith said.

Don spotted a control panel set into the wall—clearly identifiable, even though its design was unusual. He went to it and input the security codes he knew, hoping for the best. He grinned, as the ship's CPU came online like it had been waiting for him. "I've got her onboard computer up . . . Whoa!" he breathed, staring at the displays.

"Not working?" Robinson asked him, coming alongside.

"No, it's working, all right. It's just, I don't know, too damn fast—" He shook his head again as lights flickered to life along the corridor, illuminating the way ahead. The robot rolled past them, and he followed with the rest.

Back aboard the *Jupiter*, Will watched his monitor in fascination, seeing through the robot's eyes as the away team moved deeper into the strange ship. He glanced down as the audio light began to blink on his display panel, and touched the volume control. He listened, half frowning, as he heard something that sounded like dripping. "Dad," he said into the microphone, "do you . . ."

". . . *hear something?*" the robot asked, echoing Will's query to its human followers. It turned and started on again, and as they followed, the sound of dripping grew louder ahead.

"Like the drip, drip, drip of blood . . ." Smith murmured.

Don looked back at him; Smith's mouth quirked in satisfaction.

"You really need to shut up," Don muttered, feeling his face flush as he looked away again.

"Here." Robinson stopped up ahead, and pointed at the ceiling.

Don glanced up, and saw the hole: It looked as though the ceiling had been chewed away, by something with unimaginable teeth. There was a service tunnel overhead, barely visible through some kind of viscous membrane that stretched across the jagged opening from one side to the other. The membrane was dripping steadily onto the floor in front of them.

Judy stepped closer to the drip, holding out her remote to take a reading. She studied the data that came up on its displays. "That material appears to be biological."

Smith grunted. "Nothing good will come of *this*," he said.

Don glared at him. "You, of course, being the expert on space exploration."

Smith met his gaze, unsmiling. "Trust me, Major. Evil knows evil."

Don started on abruptly, cursing Smith under his breath, cursing himself for letting that psychopath get on his nerves. The others followed silently; each of them making a careful detour around the dripping membrane, and the widening puddle on the floor.

As they moved on, the ship lit up the way ahead as if

it had expected them. The blast door at the corridor's end opened silently, inviting them to pass through into another empty, well-lit space. "Motion sensors are still working," Judy observed, whispering now.

At the far end of the room Don saw another blast door, sitting partway open, as if it had jammed. This time the metal was twisted and scorched, like it had been hit by weapons-fire. Don touched the damaged door cautiously. "Plasma burns."

No one made any remarks this time, even Smith.

Don pushed through the partially open door, the others following one by one. The robot came last, prying the door wide with its powerful arms.

The passageway beyond held rows of storage lockers, and every locker held a robot. Don stopped, looking back at their own robot, looking again at the models that lined the corridor like bizarre suits of armor. Every one of them was clearly some advanced model, more versatile and sophisticated in design than anything he had seen.

Behind him Smith looked at their own robot with speculative disdain. "Well, well, aren't we the poor cousin?" he said, as if the robot cared. Or maybe he wasn't talking to the robot.

Robinson was moving down the row of lockers, studying their occupants with single-minded interest. "Rambler-Krane series robots . . ." He could have been talking to himself. "But like no design I've ever seen."

Don moved on restlessly to the far end of the corridor, where the blast doors were lodged wide-open. He looked through, and at last saw what he'd been aching to see: a control room. "Down here!" he called, and went inside.

One look around told him this was too small to be the bridge. It must have been an auxiliary operations post; there must be a lot of them, on a ship this size. But he would have given anything to see what it had looked like before it had become a battle zone.

He stared at the walls scored by laser bursts, the sections of console where the control panel had been blown completely away. The rest of the team came through and stopped, one by one, staring like he had.

Don glanced down at his environmental suit. His was military issue, designed for use with specialized equipment in combat situations. But the others were wearing ordinary fieldsuits, without all the cybernetic bells and whistles . . . without the added protection.

He looked up again, hoping the differences stayed a moot point. "It's a Remote Ops station. Looks like some kind of firefight."

Robinson moved to the com and studied the instrument arrays. "Could this ship be some sort of prototype?" he murmured. He touched something on the panel and the power came up, lighting the displays. "The Captain's log has degraded. Maybe I can gather some fragments." His hands moved over the panel with studied efficiency. "Wait . . . here we go." He looked up, as the main display screen came alive.

Don watched the screen fill with static snow. Gradually he made out a human face, saw the features begin to granulate in as the computer erased the electronic noise from the image. In the background, the *Proteus*'s bridge was becoming visible, its crew moving back and forth in normal shipboard activity; the image alternated with a surface view of the planet they were orbiting.

Don studied the emerging face of the Captain again, and his breath caught. "Jeb," he whispered. *It was Jeb . . . it couldn't be anyone else.* He crossed the room to get closer to the screen, everyone and everything else forgotten. *But . . . but—*

"The hyperspace tracker seems to be functioning," Jeb was saying. His face wavered and for a moment the words dissolved into static. ". . . No sign of the *Jupiter Two* . . ." The image faded, ". . . have exceeded our timetable . . ." faded again, ". . . I'm not willing to give up."

For one moment the image became perfectly clear, and Don had the uncanny sense that the man on the screen looked straight into his eyes. "Don would keep looking for me." *It was Jeb.*

But the shaven head he remembered so well had grown a shock of cropped black hair . . . and Jeb had a mustache . . . there were even laugh lines starting at the corners of his eyes. *As if somehow Jeb had aged half a decade overnight.*

Don looked away, rubbing his eyes. When he looked back, there was only static on the screen.

"That's it," Robinson said. "The rest of the data is totally corrupted."

Robinson didn't look like someone who'd just seen a man age half a decade in a day. But then, Robinson didn't know Jeb . . .

But anyway, that was impossible! All of this had to be impossible . . . didn't it? "How could they launch a rescue mission for us when we've only been lost a day?" Don asked, and his own voice sounded like a stranger's.

Nobody answered him; Robinson shook his head.

"Looks like they brought something up from the planet's surface," Judy said, from the Life Sciences console. "Got it . . ."

A blurred holograph appeared above the panel, rotating slowly; the degraded image of a peculiar viscous pouch. "It's some sort of egg sack."

It seemed to be alive, quivering . . . It reminded him somehow of the dripping membrane they'd seen in the corridor. He looked back over his shoulder at the way they'd come; noticed suddenly that Smith was not in the room. "Smith!" he shouted furiously, starting for the door. "Get back here!"

Smith reappeared in the doorway before Don could finish crossing the room. "Happy to oblige, Major." Smith smiled, glancing upward, away from Don's angry face. "Although I don't think it's *me* you should be worrying about. But rather, these . . ." He pointed at the ceiling.

Don looked up. In the ceiling overhead there were rows and rows of membrane-covered holes.

Across the room the robot came alive and said, *"I'm detecting motion. Behind you—"*

Don turned back just in time to see a towering shadow-form shoot past another doorway.

"After it," Robinson said. "Move! Bring Smith," he told the robot, as they ran out the door.

Don raced down the corridor, and into another world. Flowering vines tendrilled along its walls, becom-

ing more thickly matted as he went farther. More vines
wove a twisted carpet over the metal floor, muffling his
steps.

The foliage grew ever denser, until by the time he
finally reached another doorway he was forcing his way
through heavy brush. Beyond the doorway was a rain
forest. He stopped, staring around him at the rampant
overabundance of nature that had somehow flourished
here, in the heart of a deserted starship countless light-
years from Earth.

"Hydroponics," Robinson said, as the others joined him.

"Growth like this would take decades," Judy murmured.

Don thought of Jeb, looking half a decade older. And
this ship—this level of tech made the *Jupiter* look like a
biplane . . . No way did the ASOMAC he knew possess
this kind of technology. Only a starship run by a waking
crew on long interstellar voyages would need a hydroponics lab. . . .

How had the probe ship even followed them here,
when *they* didn't even know where the hell they were?
He vaguely remembered the older Jeb in the starship's
log saying something about a "hyperspace tracker."

But that would mean the *Proteus* had a way to navi-
gate the hyperspace wormholes without a gate.

My God . . . He didn't say anything, as the robot
arrived in the lab, dragging Smith in one claw.

"Unhand me, you mechanical moron," Smith said
through gritted teeth.

Don felt a smile start; looked past Smith as a subtle
movement in the leaves caught his eye. "Don't move."

He plunged his gauntleted hand into the bushes, felt it close over something that was neither leaf nor vine—something alive and struggling. Leaves flew as he dragged the thing back out of the bushes into the light.

The creature he held stared wildly back at him with enormous deep-blue eyes. *It looked like a cat . . . or a teddy bear . . . no, more like a monkey, with those ears . . . only its skin was spiny like a tiny dragon's . . .* As he watched, its skin began to change color, mottling from leafy green toward the black of his fieldsuit . . . *Like a chameleon?*

"Excellent!" the robot said, as Will gave the creature a thumbs-up. The robot released Smith from its grasp.

The squirming creature was entirely the color of his fieldsuit now, as if it only wanted to disappear from sight. As if it was terrified of him.

Don held it more gently. "Easy there, little buddy," he murmured. "No one's going to hurt you." He began to stroke the creature's head, as if it was a cat. He'd always been good with animals . . . better than he was with people, usually.

To his surprise, it stopped struggling and began to croon softly. *It actually liked that.* Then it began to emit small *blawps* of contentment, the way a cat might purr. Slowly, its color brightened to a golden-yellow.

"Looks like you've made a friend," Judy said, smiling at him.

His own smile widened.

"Still . . . I'd hold off a couple of weeks before getting her name tattooed on your arm." She moved on past him to study a fern.

He looked down at the creature clinging to the front of his fieldsuit, so that he didn't have to look at her. "Do yourself a favor," he muttered. "Don't evolve."

"How charming," Smith said witheringly. "Doctor Dolittle of outer space."

"It's possible this is one of the creatures from the alien ship," Robinson remarked, pulling absently at his beard, as if none of their general conversation occurred in a range audible to him.

The alien climbed Don's arm with four-fingered, suckered hands and feet. It clung to his equipment harness, burying its tiny face against his neck. He laughed in surprise, stroking its back. "It looks like a child."

Smith grimaced. "If so, my dear Major . . . what do you suppose happened to its parents?"

They looked at him. "Let's get back to Remote Ops," Robinson said.

As they started toward the doorway, Don saw Robinson hesitate a moment and glance back into the canopy of foliage. But there was nothing to see up there. Don shrugged. The faint rustling that seemed to follow them was only leaves moving in the breeze of their passage . . . *Wasn't it?*

Back at Remote Ops, Robinson headed directly to the com and checked its displays. "I've tapped into the internal sensor array," he said. "Besides us, this ship is totally deserted."

"A ghost ship," Smith muttered again.

Don ignored him this time, preoccupied with the tiny

alien still clinging to his suit. Was it really a child . . . an orphan? Or only a pet? How long had it been here, all alone? How could you judge the intelligence of an alien life-form, when it was *alien* . . . ?

He sat down and unsealed a pocket flap with his free hand. Baby or pet, there were some things every living creature needed. Digging out one of his ration bars, he turned it over. "And the flavor of the day is . . . *banana/beef.*" He made a face. "Who thinks up these combinations?"

The creature watched intently as he tore open the foil. Its eyes were enormous; they reminded him of a fairy tale he'd heard as a child, about a dog with eyes as large as plates. He took a bite of the food bar, chewing loudly. "Mmm. Good," he said. From the corner of his eye he saw a reluctant smile come out on Judy's face.

"Major West, I highly recommend you never breed," Smith said. "That, by the way, is my medical opinion."

Don frowned, and offered his food to the tiny alien. It fingered the pouch, emitted a small *blawp*, and took a tentative bite from the food bar. Its eyes widened further than he would have believed possible, and it ate the whole bar, wrapper and all. "Little thing was hungry," he said, with a satisfied smile.

"Good Lord, who will spare us the tyranny of the sentimental?" Smith turned away, as if the sight of them was more than he could bear.

Somewhere in the distance a high-pitched whine began, making the air vibrate faintly around them.

"I don't like the sound of that sound . . ." Judy said.

Don glanced at the com, at the telltale signs of a firefight. *What really happened to the* Proteus's *crew—?*

The tiny alien began to scream; it leaped out of Don's arms, landing on Smith's back, clinging to his neck, still shrieking.

"Get this infernal creature off me!" Smith shouted, trying to slap it loose.

Judy pulled the shrieking alien off him; it buried its face against her, changing colors, trying to disappear into her suit as the whine grew louder.

The noise seemed to be coming from above them now. Don looked up. The rows of membrane-covered holes were trembling, distorting as though something— no, *things*, a lot of them, were trying to push their way through.

Ghost ship . . . ? Don reached for his gun.

Chapter Thirteen

On the *Jupiter Two*'s bridge, Maureen Robinson wiped sweat from her forehead and peered down into the entrails of the sensor console again. She and Penny had spent the time since the away team had gone out working to get the last of their damaged information systems back online, while Will watched over the others' progress through the robot's eyes. This was a job that had to be finished before they could make sense of the data coming in; and it kept their minds off other things.

Why is it you never have a hairpin when you need one? Maureen thought irritably. She had tried everything else to repair this damn connection. At least the ship had been well stocked with replacement components: Like the iron men in wooden ships who had sailed Earth's seas for centuries, the *Jupiter*'s crew had to be able to fend for themselves in an emergency far from home ... *Hah. Got it.* She smiled.

Penny looked up from rewiring the final monitor and said, "Try it now."

Maureen activated the console; the displays came alive, showing her all green, indicating the system was fully operational at last. Maureen smiled at her daughter and gave her an appreciative nod. She looked down at the displays again as the data she'd been waiting for began to fill the screens. "Strange . . ." She studied the infrared image of the *Proteus*'s outer hull, the peculiar patches of scales on its smooth metallic skin. "Those scales are giving off heat."

Penny came to stand beside her, looking at the screen, her forehead furrowing.

"Give me an external view," Maureen said. Penny input the command. Their view of the *Proteus* widened, until they could see the *Jupiter Two* beside it in space. As they watched, the silver disks on the hull of the probe ship began to move, stirring like crustaceans disturbed by an unseen tide: *They were alive . . .*

One by one they rose up on spindly crablike legs . . . *No, not like crabs. Like spiders. Spiders in armor.* Maureen watched in horrified fascination as the aliens skittered silently over the *Proteus*'s hull.

And began to disappear, one by one. She realized now that what had appeared to be the starship's seamless ceralloy hull was actually riddled with holes, each one covered by some sort of living membrane. *They were going into the ship.* "John," she breathed, "get the hell out of there . . ."

The tiny alien's shrieking reached new heights of hysteria as a shape began to push through the membranous hole in the ceiling.

Don drew his gun as the membrane excreted a techo-organic monster. It dropped to the floor in front of them, a living machine with a metal carapace supported on translucent spidery limbs. A taloned whip of tail lashed the air like a scorpion's stinger. Binocular protrusions on what he guessed was a head swiveled toward him, reminding him eerily of the mindless eyes of a 3D cam. *Eyes* ...

More spider-aliens were pushing through the membrane, thudding to the floor behind it. Abruptly the thing in front of him scuttled toward him and sprang, its razor-edged maw gaping, *as if it wanted to be the first to—*

Don jerked his gun up and fired.

The laser bolt refracted harmlessly off the thing's metallic torso. The alien clanged to the floor, retracting its limbs and eyes as the impact of the shot knocked it spinning back into the mass of spiders.

"Out!" John shouted. "Now!"

Don fled with the rest back down the corridor that led to the airlock. The spider-things poured into the hallway after them, ricocheting and rebounding off walls and floor as though gravity didn't exist, while more monsters dropped down through the ceiling above their heads.

On the bridge of the *Jupiter Two*, Will worked frantically at his keyboard, making his robot the last line of defense for his father's fleeing team. "These controls are too slow!" He shoved away from the keyboard. "Activate holographic interface." A virtual simulacrum of the robot appeared in the center of the room. He stepped inside it, and the image synchronized with his motion. He spun, facing backward, and fired its weapon simulators.

Aboard the *Proteus* the actual robot swiveled on its treads, following Will's motion, to fire on the pursuing spiders. The laser bursts of its arc welders had more effect than Don's pistol, blasting aliens into bits of flesh and shrapnel. But through its sensors he could see even more spiders pouring out of the ceiling to replace them.

And he saw some of them lag behind, stopping beside the wounded spiders flailing brokenly on the floor. *Were they helping each other, like humans?*

As he watched through the robot's eyes, the spiders fell on their wounded comrades and began to rip them limb from limb, devouring them alive.

Will gave a squawk of sickened disbelief that made his mother and sister turn. "They *eat* their wounded!"

"They eat their wounded!"

Was that what the robot had said? Don slowed his headlong flight down the corridor, trying to see past the robot's massive body to what was happening behind them.

"Duck!" Judy shouted suddenly. He looked ahead again, saw her take aim—straight at him. He dove for the floor as she fired her pulse rifle, hitting the fire sensor panel beside the open blast door. The door slammed shut just behind the robot, crushing spider bodies with a grinding *crunch*.

Don scrambled to his feet. Emergency lighting stained

the tunnel a bloody crimson. He saw the others slow down and then stop up ahead. He looked where they were looking. The blast door at the other end of the tunnel had closed at the same time, sealing them off from the airlock access.

They were trapped.

He leaned against the wall, panting; watched the others search the suddenly claustrophobic space with frightened eyes as they realized the same thing.

The spiders ate their wounded. Alive. He knew now why there had been no trace of the *Proteus*'s crew. *Was this how it had ended for Jeb?*

"We've got to get that door open," Robinson said. He started on toward the far end of the corridor. The others followed him without a word, as if they didn't know what else to do.

Don started after them, knowing it was futile, wondering when they would figure that out. No one could open a blast door, once the locks were set. But the spiders could eat their way through anything on this ship. It was only a matter of time before they ate their way in here . . . He slowed, and stopped, midway down the corridor. Closed his eyes, and saw Jeb's face.

And then he knew what he was going to do.

He went down on one knee, facing back the way they had come. "A million bucks' worth of *weaponry*—" he muttered, slamming a pulse enhancer onto the barrel of his gun, "—and I'd trade it *all*—" he engaged the wrist support, "for a lousy *can of Raid*."

He hit a stud on his jacket control panel, enabling the blast shield on the helmet of his fieldsuit. It rose like a cobra's hood from the yoke of his equipment harness; segmented alloy shields fanned down to cover his face.

Kneeling there, he waited, his eyes fixed on the door. The metal was already beginning to buckle.

At the far end of the corridor Judy watched her father carry on his electronic debate with the door's control panel, telling herself that if anyone could convince it to let them pass, her father could.

The small alien clung to her neck like a frightened baby, pulling at her hair. She winced, removed its tiny clutching fingers and set it down on the floor; trying not to lose her temper with it just because it was being so difficult, so impossible, *so much like the damned door that she had so stupidly sealed shut on them*—

She looked back as an earsplitting burst of sound echoed toward them: pulse weapon fire. She saw Don West, kneeling in the hellshine of the emergency lights far down the tunnel, firing back the way they had come. And then she saw the spiders . . .

The tiny alien covered its enormous eyes with its ears, huddling in the corner by her feet.

"I can't override the fire protocols," her father said.

As Judy turned back in dismay, the robot suddenly came to life behind her. *"Stand clear,"* it said. She scooped up the alien baby, pushing the others with her as she moved out of the way.

The robot settled itself like a runner digging in, and raised its grappling arms. An energy charge began to build, crackling between its pincer claws, and she had to remind herself that this time it was really Will telling them to get clear, her own brother who controlled the robot's weapons—

Who sent it barreling forward at top speed, and fired an energy blast just as it crashed into the immovable door, blowing a hole through the ceralloy that left it torn and seared. As the others pushed forward she looked back, shouting, "Don—!"

Don glanced back over his shoulder as he heard the explosion. He saw the glowing hole in the blast door; thought he saw someone waving him toward it.

And then he looked ahead again, and went on killing spiders.

He was dimly aware that the others were escaping, dimly aware that he should go with them. But he couldn't go yet . . . the spiders kept coming and coming; they'd eaten through the door, and too many of them were still coming at him . . . not enough of them were piled up dead yet in front of him. *There would never be enough dead spiders, even if he went on blasting them until the end of time. They had killed his best friend, and he would—he was . . .*

He was alone. The team was gone, and suddenly there were no more monsters coming through the door.

He staggered to his feet in the sudden silence; lowered his aching arms, his numb hands barely keeping hold of his weapon. Blue-black ichor dripped from his suit and helmet. He looked over his shoulder and then back down the splattered, reeking tunnel. Spider guts and spider shrapnel were piled knee-deep in front of him in the lurid glare.

"No way it's that easy," he mumbled, shaking his head. He looked again at the glowing hole in the far door: *the way out, waiting for him ...*

And then he looked back, one more time. And watched the floor in front of him begin to heave and rise, throwing off the midden of fragmented spider parts. ...

A giant's shadow fell across his shielded face as he stood frozen in disbelief, looking up, and up ... as the mother of all Alien-Monster-Spider-Things rose before him like a cresting wave.

"Oh, *shi*—" Don raised his gun and fired, point-blank, blowing it to hell and gone as he staggered back out of range.

It was gone, all right. Leaving a gaping hole in the corridor floor . . . freeing countless techno-organic drones to come swarming up through the gap in a hideous flood. They poured endlessly out of the floor from somewhere down below *to surround him and smother him and tear the flesh from his living body*—

Don threw himself backward as they flowed around him; shoulder-rolled, blasting spiders mindlessly as he scrambled to his feet again. He bolted down the corridor, freed now of the killing fury that had made even his own survival meaningless. The seething avalanche of spiders flowed after him in a single undulating mass, covering walls and floor and ceiling, gaining on him with every heartbeat. *God, they were fast! Damn it, why hadn't he seen how long this tunnel really was—?*

They were almost on him, he had seconds left, but he was almost to the blast door, *almost there, almost*—

As he leaped for the opening, the spider at his heels whipped its taloned tail forward. He jagged, barely dodging the meathook at its tip . . . lost his footing, and fell.

Maureen ran to the com as she heard her husband's voice call her name. She saw him onscreen through the robot's eyes, standing at the airlock door, inputting codes while the others waited tensely behind him. *An airlock. Then they were almost safe*—

John looked up from the panel access; he spread his hands in frustration. *The lock wasn't responding.* "Maureen, can you give me something—?"

She queried the *Proteus*'s CPU, found the answer she needed. "It's cycling through a vacuum check. I'm overriding. Try it now. John—?" She looked up again when he didn't answer. The screen where she had seen his face was empty.

Don fell headlong through the ruined blast door, into the airlock access. He landed hard, gasping with pain as the fall knocked the wind out of him.

The monster lunged after him from the other side, its serrated maw opening wide as it saw him stranded on the floor, helpless, fresh meat—

Suddenly, his front-row view of his own death was blotted out by a fluid wall of blue: The robot stood before him, barricading the door with its back.

The Robinson home in future Houston.

Dr. John Robinson introduces Dr. Judy Robinson to Major Don West.

Dr. Zachary Smith.

Jupiter 2's launch.

Jupiter 2 *and the* Proteus.

Searching the Proteus.

The spiders attack!

The Robot in action.

Blawp with Penny Robinson.

Jupiter 2 *crashlanding on the planet.*

Don and Judy get better acquainted.

First look at the new planet.

Older Will.

Future Smith.

Will with the re-built Robot.
Escape through the self-destructing planet.

Metal clanged on metal; the robot's body shuddered like a human's, but it did not give way as the spider-things mounted a savage, single-minded attack from the other side of the doorway. Don heard the wrenching squeal of metal, as teeth that could rip a starship open like a can of tuna tore into the robot's back. He tried to get his feet under him, desperate to get away from the door and what lay beyond it, but his body seemed to have turned to rubber.

Abruptly there were hands under his shoulders, lifting him up, helping him stand. He turned, and saw Judy, her eyes shining with relief and—

"Let's move!" Robinson called. The lights went green, the door slid open; and suddenly there was no time for him to say anything to Judy, even if he could have found the words.

Judy let him go, and they ran for it with the rest.

Chapter Fourteen

Maureen and Penny sat at the com of the *Jupiter Two*, powering up the ship's drive. Behind them Will fought virtual monsters, heaving invisible spiders off the back of his sim, as the real robot fought real monsters at the other end of their link. Its holographic form around him was already flickering in places, as the real-time damage to the robot mounted.

"Will," his father shouted from the *Proteus*'s airlock, "can you get the robot in here?"

More spiders clung to its hull, burrowing through its body in their mindless urge to destroy the living flesh it was keeping from them. Will grimaced as if he could actually feel its pain, and shook his head. "I can't move him without letting the spiders into the ship!" The robot was crawling with them, inside and out; they were pushing through gaping rents in its body, furiously trying to reach the humans in the airlock.

"Leave him behind," his father ordered, and Will could barely see the emotion on his face.

"I'm sorry . . ." Will whispered his final words to the robot, and began to disengage the simbot's controls.

*   *   *

On board the *Proteus*, a spider squeezed through the robot's ruined body, flinging itself with monomaniacal bloodlust toward the airlock door.

"Seal it! Now!" Robinson shouted, and Don hit the button with his fist. The door was still closing as the first monster reached them. The spider thing lashed out, grazing Smith's back with its taloned whip, just as the door dropped down.

The alien baby leaped from Judy's arms with a shriek of terror, landed on Smith, and launched itself toward the rear of the chamber. The door sealed shut, lopping off the alien's tailhook. It dropped with a mucasoid *splat* to the floor in the sudden silence of their profound relief.

Smith rubbed his back, glaring at the trembling form of the alien baby huddled again in Judy's arms. "This tiny horror scratched me."

Don pressed the stud on his jacket with an unsteady hand, finally retracting the blast shield and his helmet. He looked down, his heart beating like a fist against his ribs as he stared at the severed appendage still twitching on the floor. Slowly, the lock cycled.

Back on board the *Jupiter Two*, Don shoved his way past the others, heading for his chair at the com. He sank into the pilot's seat—*his seat*—with a sense of stupefying gratitude. And then he looked at the screens. The exterior view of both ships showed him countless spiders emerging from the *Proteus*, swarming over its hull to the place where the *Jupiter* was docked.

Robinson took the copilot's seat. "Prepare to disengage," he said; but Don was already there.

*   *   *

Will watched from inside the simbot as his father and Major West went to the com without a backward glance. More pieces of the robot's image winked out around him with every passing second.

He stepped out of the mangled form, no longer able to go on witnessing its horrible death. "Good-bye, Robot," he whispered.

Penny came up beside him and put her arm around his shoulders. "You couldn't save him, kid," she murmured.

Will looked up, seeing his sister's face haloed by a sudden flash of inspiration. "Save him—" he said. "Of course!" He ran to the console and shoved a microdisk into his deck. He ordered the robot's memory to download, his fingers flying over the keys. The monitor lit up in front of him, showing him the progress of his save: 75% . . . 80% . . . The screen went blank, and DOWNLOAD INCOMPLETE flashed across it. His face fell. Penny sighed, shaking her head, and turned away to her work station.

As she sat down, a small blur came shooting past Will and skittered up the back of her chair—over her head, tangling itself in her hair, before it landed in a heap in her lap.

"Are you insane?" Penny shouted furiously. "Look at my hair!" Wiping her hair back from her face, she looked down—and found the alien baby huddled on her lap. Its scaled skin rippled through rainbows of color until it was the exact shade of her clothes. She gave a small laugh of amazement and gently touched its face.

Chapter
Fifteen

Don released the docking ring. He looked up, watching the monitors as the *Jupiter Two* drifted free from the probe ship's side. An endless stream of spiders was still pouring out of the *Proteus*. His stomach knotted. "This is a fun picnic," he muttered, forcing his gaze away from the screens. "First yellow aliens, now giant spiders." Across the room the tiny alien buried its face against Penny's chest.

"It's okay. Everything's going to be all right . . ." Penny murmured. Her voice sounded anything but certain.

"We're clear. Everybody hang on." Don did a controlled burn of the *Jupiter*'s engines, boosting them away from the probe ship. The spiders bounded down the *Proteus*'s hull in a frantic mob as the gap of empty space between the two ships widened.

Don grinned in satisfaction, watching their frenzied disappointment. "And the crowd goes wild—"

"Recall your nightmares from childhood, Major," Smith said, with heavy skepticism. "Monsters are rarely so easily dissuaded."

Don looked down at his ichor-smeared clothing. His hands twitched. He swiveled his chair to face Smith.

"Why don't you go out and talk to them then, Smith?
Bug to bug."

Smith's mouth twisted. "I think they'd rather come
inside." He nodded at the screens.

Don turned back, and breathed a curse. Uncountable
numbers of spiders covered the *Proteus*'s skin like blood-
sucking lice, a parasitic infestation of monsters. As he
watched, they began to hurl themselves from the probe
ship's surface; launching into space, legs retracted, they
spun like silver disks toward the *Jupiter*'s retreating
hull . . .

"Arming torpedoes—" Don input the commands.
"Fire in the hole!"

An array of rockets shot out into the swirling mass of
spiders. He watched, holding his breath, waiting for the
fireworks as they detonated.

The torpedoes flared up and went dead, like defective
birthday candles, drifting through the sea of spiders and
on into the darkness without killing even one. Don
slammed his fist down on his seat arm.

"The robot must have damaged the detonator cores,"
Robinson said. "They won't blow."

Don turned back to the monitors, feeling the unfa-
miliar tingle of panic in his gut as he watched the spider
swarm close with the ship. Some of them overshot. Others made it, reextending their limbs, and began to bur-
row into the hull.

And then the ones on the ship began to shoot filaments of webbing from their bellies, catching the strag-
glers and reeling them in.

Maureen Robinson came back onto the bridge from

belowdecks with the severed tail held in metal tongs. She carried it to the Life Sciences console.

"That's the same expression you had when my mother came to stay with us," John said.

She threw him a mildly scandalized look. "DNA extrapolation coming up now."

A graphic of the severed appendage appeared in Don's lower monitor; he watched as the computer extrapolated an image of the whole thing, filling in muscles and flesh.

"Silicon based," Maureen said. "Adamantium shell and lack of respiratory system suggest an ability to live in deep space. Tiny front brain implies communal relationships. Like bees."

Or army ants, Don thought. Nothing seemed to stop them, not even hard vacuum. They just kept coming. He looked away from the screen. "If the biology lesson is over, Professor, I could use some *help* here—"

Maureen glanced up at him. "If you can't find what hurts an enemy, Major," she said evenly, "find what it loves." She nodded at the displays on her console. "They may be attracted to heat and light."

Heat and light. That was why they'd followed the Jupiter *out into space. That was why they went after living flesh ...*

He turned back to the control panel, and began to input commands. The *Jupiter* wasn't the only ship with a functioning drive unit. Their computer was still linked to the one on board the *Proteus.* If he played this just right—

The screens told him the *Proteus* was responding, powering up on cue; he saw her tubes glowing red as the engines began their initial burn. "Remote commands are working," he said. "I'm bringing the fusion drive on line."

"*Warning*," the computer said. "*Outer hull has been compromised.*"

He looked up at the screen, at the spiders slowly flensing the ship's skin.

The *Proteus*'s drive ignited; a few spiders still drifting from silks behind the *Jupiter* broke free, heading back toward the probe ship. Most of them stayed.

"Let's turn up the heat—" He headed the *Jupiter* back toward the *Proteus*, aiming directly for the wake of the fusion drives.

"*Warning*," the computer said. "*Inner hull breach in twenty seconds.*"

Don glanced irritably at Robinson. "You invent that too?"

"Uh . . . yes, actually," Robinson said.

"Can you *shut it up*?" Don turned back to the com, wiping sweat from his forehead.

He cut straight through the *Proteus*'s nuclear wake; felt an electric jolt of elation as the spiders abandoned the *Jupiter* in droves. He watched their spiraling flight back toward the probe ship, where they attached themselves to the superheated nacelles of the drive. He glanced at the displays. *All of them. It got every one.*

Now they were just where he wanted them.

Don began to feed more commands to the probe ship's CPU.

"What are you doing?" Robinson asked, as if he had followed every step easily, until now.

"Never leave an enemy stronghold intact," Don said. "One of your father's first rules of engagement." He hit a button. On the displays that showed him the *Proteus*'s operating systems, something began to flash: FUSION DRIVE OVERLOAD. He didn't bother to explain it.

"Major, stop—" Robinson said, his voice turning angry.

Don ignored him, went on locking in the commands. *Jeb going down under that swarming mass of monsters, to be ripped to pieces . . . Jaws, gaping above him . . .* The images echoed like a scream in his brain.

The spiders had to die. He had to kill them. Every single one of them. It was his responsibility to make sure they never did to another innocent being what they'd done to Jeb. What they'd almost done to him. *It was his right—*

"That's a direct order!" Robinson's hand closed like a vise on his arm; he shrugged it off. "We might need to salvage—"

Don hit a button. OVERLOAD shone on his displays like a star. "*I hate spiders*," he said.

The *Jupiter*'s thrusters kicked in, punching them out of their orbital duet with the *Proteus* as the probe ship's engines began to glow with an unhealthy light. He threw everything the *Jupiter*'s drive had into putting space—a lot of space—between her and the *Proteus*. He watched the probe ship diminish on his screens; watched the pulsing glow spread along its entire length as the nuclear core went critical.

The ship began to vent plasma like a diseased sun; superheated gases spiraled out into the darkness. He kept his eyes riveted on the screens, aware of nothing else now, not even the expression on his face.

The *Proteus* exploded spectacularly, going up like a nova in silent splendor, and in his mind he pictured countless spiders vaporized inside the inferno of raging plasma . . .

Don sat blinking as if he'd forgotten how to see; his vision cleared and he found himself back on the *Jupiter*'s bridge. The *Proteus* was gone. He looked up at the monitors, expecting to see nothing but starry night.

Instead he saw a glowing shell of superheated plasma expanding outward from the explosion, roaring toward them at a fraction of the speed of light. He looked at the displays. "That's coming really fast, isn't it . . . ?" he said.

Robinson stared at him as if he'd gone insane; turned away furiously, shouting, "Gravity harnesses! Now!"

Don input the emergency command sequence. The console split open, giving him access to the manual helm controls. Smith bolted for a seat at an empty work station, as localized fields of artificial gravity pulled the crew down into their chairs and held them fast.

The shock wave hit the *Jupiter Two* like a fly swatter taking out a gnat, and sent them hurtling out of control toward the nameless planet lying below.

Don never remembered how long it took him to throw off the brain-bruising vertigo of the impact and stabilize their plummeting dive toward the surface. The *Jupiter* fought gallantly to answer his commands, but he knew they'd run out of luck the instant the shock wave had hurled them into the gravity well. The *Jupiter Two* had never been meant to enter an atmosphere; there was nothing aerodynamic about her design. She flew like a stone.

This ship would never taste vacuum again, he thought. This camping trip would be over when they hit the ground; the only thing still up to him was whether they all ended it in one piece.

The *Jupiter* plunged through the cloud layer, and a driving blizzard whited out the viewport.

"Pull up. *Pull up!*" John Robinson shouted in his ear. Don remembered abruptly that he was not alone.

"Really? No kidding? Thanks." He glared at Robinson. *Genius. Right.*

He looked back out the viewport, and gasped a curse as the clouds parted: The range of mountains dead ahead looked like a glittering sawblade, and its peaks were a hell of a lot closer to heaven than they were right now.

He banked the *Jupiter* hard, feeling the ship respond with agonizing reluctance. They seemed to perform the maneuver in slow motion, yawing ninety degrees to port just in time to split the air between two fangs of stone, cutting through a glacier-eaten pass as they followed their headlong trajectory toward the planet's surface.

"I'm reading a clearing ahead," he said hoarsely. "Hang on! It's gonna be a bumpy landing—"

The *Jupiter Two* blew over a carpet of what looked like snow-laden trees. Its underside kissed the canopy; treetops burst into flames with the blistering friction of its passage. He felt more than heard the *Jupiter* lose pieces of its skin as the branches flayed its hull.

They cleared the trees, barely fifty meters above the

ground, and he saw the clearing the sensors had indi-
cated. It was an enormous impact crater, filled with
water.

Not the kind of landing field he'd been praying for.
But all the landing field he was going to get. He'd have
to make do . . . He set the controls and braced against
the panel, felt a cry of defiance and sheer exhilaration
rise in his throat as the surface rushed up to meet him.

The *Jupiter Two* hit the water and skimmed its surface
like a stone—skipping once, twice, three times across the
alien sea, barely slowing down. "Hang on!" Don shouted,
and took his own advice. The ship plowed into the
far shore, smashing through snow-covered boulders and
vegetation, finally grinding to a halt among the rocks
below the crater wall.

Everything was dark and still when John opened his
eyes. In the dim glow of the emergency lights he could
see automatic fire systems hissing on and off, releasing
controlled bursts of chemical foam. *At least they were
working this time.*

This time . . . He raised his hands to his head. Crisis
overlaid disaster in his memory until time had no meaning. Everything about this mission . . . about their very
lives . . . had been hurled completely off the map. They
had seen, and survived, so many impossible things in less
than a day that he could barely believe he was still alive—
let alone that not even twenty-four hours had passed.

He pushed himself up; his eyes searched the room. If
anything had happened to his family . . . *My God*, he

thought, overwhelmed by a sickening wave of despair. *What hasn't happened?*

But he couldn't let himself drown. He was responsible for everything that had happened. He had to be strong, he had to get past any weakness and fear. His family was depending on him.

And not just his family. The success of this mission, the survival of the human race.

He had to stay in control. His father would.

Don West sat up, rubbing his face; the others were beginning to stir. John released his harness. "Everybody, by the numbers," he called; steadying himself and, he hoped, them with the emergency drill they had practiced together for so long.

Maureen straightened up in her seat, rubbing her neck. "Life Science, still breathing."

"Mission medical," Judy said. "I'm alive."

"Me too," Will chimed. "Robotics, I mean."

"Video Mechanics, okay," Penny reported, still clutching the small alien in her arms.

"I'm alive," Smith said, though John hadn't asked, and didn't care. "Major West's poor excuse for piloting skills notwithstanding."

"Let's take a look—" West said, stubbornly ignoring them both as he turned his seat toward the com.

John imagined how his father would have dealt with someone as defiantly insubordinate as West; his jaw tightened until it ached.

West hit some button on the control panel, de-icing the ship's viewport to give them their first real look at the new world.

"Ah, Dorothy..." Smith said acidly, "back in Kansas at last."

Before them lay the crater's snow-covered floor, and the sea that it encompassed. The gentle arc of the crater's thirty-meter-high rim led their eyes toward a distant horizon reddened by the light of two setting suns.

A new world. But not the one they'd wanted.

John looked away, unable to see any beauty in the view, feel any awe at being here to witness it. He looked back at West.

West stared unblinkingly into the sunset. John wondered what the man could possibly be feeling; whether he had even the slightest idea how much his actions had cost them all.

If he didn't know now, he was going to find out, soon enough.

Chapter
Sixteen

"**You violated** a direct order—"

Don pushed off from the cold outcrop of rock where he had been sitting alone and walked away, shutting Robinson's words, and their meaning, out of his mind. Above him the moonless sky was filled with an utterly alien starfield; the snowy ground of an alien world crunched beneath his boots with every step. Ahead of him, through the fog of his breath, the *Jupiter Two* lay like a beached whale below the wall of the crater.

From this distance the *Jupiter*'s enormous sheltering form looked oddly small, vulnerable. The exterior floodlights fought a lonely, losing battle against the universal darkness. Don shoved his numb hands deeper into the pockets of his parka, and headed back toward the ship.

He ducked in through the open entry hatch, took the corridor that led to Engineering. Robinson's brisk footsteps closed with his; he knew he was just postponing the inevitable.

His own footsteps echoed suddenly as he entered the cavernous space of the engine room. He slowed as he reached the shielded wall of the thruster core. The fuel cylinder lay exposed; its register was flashing HALF POWER.

Robinson reached his side and stopped. They stood together but apart, staring at the displays. He knew the sight must be putting all the same thoughts into Robinson's head that already filled his own. None of them were good.

"About half the core material is burned out," Don said finally. He kept his voice completely neutral; not acknowledging anything but Robinson's physical proximity. "We'll never generate enough power to break orbit."

"I *ordered* you not to blow that ship's reactors," Robinson said, stepping into his personal space, refusing to be ignored.

Don drifted on across the room, ignoring him anyway. "Atmospheric controls are marginal." He pointed to a display on the Engineering console. "It's gonna get cold in here tonight." He shifted position again, gesturing. "Also, the Pod and the Chariot are pretty much scrap metal." He shrugged, not making eye contact as he started back toward the entrance again.

Robinson caught up with him, jerking him back and around. "*Don't* walk away from me when I'm talking to you." Suddenly there was someone else behind Robinson's eyes: someone who had never let anyone give him static, ever; who had never cut an inch of slack, for anyone's sake.

Who the hell do you think you are, my father? Don pulled free of Robinson's grip. He backed away, shaking himself out. "Give it a rest, Professor," he said, giving the older man a shovelful of attitude. Two could play this game; and he'd been an ace by the time he was fifteen. "I was technically still in command."

"Don't hand me that!" Robinson shot back. "I'm commander of this mission."

Don smirked. "Look, no offense . . . but you're an egghead with an honorary rank. No one ever intended you to handle combat situations."

Robinson's face reddened, and he knew he'd scored a hit. "Oh, you handled it *brilliantly*, sending us crashing down here—"

"Those monsters posed a continuing threat!" His voice slipped, as he saw Jeb's face, not Robinson's: *Jeb's face, years older; Jeb's face, gouged and bleeding . . . Jeb had come after him, and Jeb had died. Jeb was the closest thing to a brother he'd ever had. And he'd just wanted to pay them back—*

"I made a judgment call," he said, his voice stone cold again and his eyes burning, "and if I have to, I'll make it again. Hell, you of all people should understand that!" *You, with the war hero father; you, with the family you love . . .* "If your father were here—"

"My father is dead," Robinson said flatly. "Killed, in one of his combat missions you admire so much. My family is on this ship," he went on, before Don could close his mouth. "And you're going to follow *my* orders, whether you agree with them or not. Is that *clear*, Major?"

"Save the speeches," Don said. "I like you—" surprised in some part of his mind to realize that he did; he liked them all. "But I'm going to do whatever *I* think it takes to ensure the success of this mission. With or without your help. Is that clear, *Professor*?" He took a step forward.

Robinson's face hardened over. Don's hands tightened into fists.

From the doorway Maureen Robinson said, "Am I interrupting something?"

Men . . . Maureen shook her head, as the two of them turned like one person to stare at her. They could have *been* one person, they were standing so close to each other now; close enough to kiss—although somehow she didn't see that happening. She had listened unnoticed through half their escalating "discussion." If she'd waited another second to speak, she could have turned a fire hose on them and they wouldn't have noticed.

"No. Really." She smiled, although she was not in the least amused. "I think you two *should* go ahead and *slug it out.*" She made little urging motions with her hands. "I mean, here we are, stranded on an alien world, and you boys want to get into a *pissing* contest. So please, go for it—" She leaned against the door frame, watching their naked faces grope for a suitable fig leaf of expression.

And then, not smiling at all, she said, "I'll have Judy down here in a heartbeat to declare you *both* unfit, and I'll take over this mission." She looked at them. "Now I don't want to hear another word from you two. Is that clear?"

"Maureen—" John started.

"Listen—" Don protested.

"*Not . . . another . . . word.*" She put her hands on her hips.

Silence fell.

"Better." She nodded. "Now, if you've finished hosing down the decks with testosterone, I suggest you come with me. I may have found a way to get us off this planet."

She turned and started back down the corridor, leaving the two men behind to stare at each other, dumbstruck. But not leaving them behind so quickly that she missed hearing Don West breathe, "Wow," and her husband answer, "Tell me about it . . ."

Two sets of footsteps were already following her.

Will sat at the console in the robot bay, smiling in satisfaction as a holographic baseball materialized in the air. Gently, he guided the spinning image onto the main monitor, where it was assimilated into the computer. He glanced at the Robot's personality task bar, illuminated on the screen, and saw its percentage increase again fractionally toward his goal of 100 percent.

Static crackled in his ears.

"Can you hear me?" he asked excitedly. "Robot?" He tuned the deck, trying new frequencies, getting more static, until—

"*Systems error,*" the Robot's synthesized voice said suddenly. "*Robot unable to locate motor controls. Unable—*"

"Calm down," Will said, trying to stay calm himself. "Your body was destroyed by the space spiders, remember?"

After a moment the Robot answered, "*Affirmative.*"

"But I saved your neural net," Will explained.

"*Warning!*" the Robot blared. "Penny, give it back! *My circuits are UNBALANCED.* Mom!"

Will input commands frantically as the Robot's voice took on a panic-stricken note. "I didn't have enough time to finish the download—" he called, trying to make it understand.

"I want more desert!" the Robot said plaintively. "*Will Robinson, what is happening to me?*"

"—so I had to finish you off with another personality! I put my mind inside of yours."

"*Ah,*" the Robot said, mollified. "*That explains this warm, fuzzy feeling when I think about baseball.* STEE-RIKE!" it bellowed enthusiastically. "He's OUT!"

Will grinned. "You think *that's* good, hang on to your diodes . . ." He conjured an ice cream cone out of thin air and studied its appearance critically. "Sprinkles," he said. Its pale green dome was instantly decorated with chocolate jimmies. "No," he said, shaking his head. "Rainbow sprinkles." The sprinkles obediently changed color. He smiled with anticipation as he fed the cone to the Robot's waiting program.

"*Woah!*" the Robot said in sudden surprise. "Pistachio! Excellent!" Will nodded, his grin widening. Ever since he could remember, he'd been the only kid he knew who liked pistachio. Now at last he'd have a friend who liked it as much as he did.

"*But . . .*" The Robot broke off.

"What?" Will asked anxiously.

"*Robot tried to destroy the Robinson family,*" it said, its synthesized voice filling with confusion and distress.

"Why did Will Robinson save Robot's personality?"

Will stared at the console in surprise. At last he said, "I guess sometimes friendship means listening to your heart, not your head." He rose from his seat, and picked up the defunct bubble diode that Penny had helped him replace. He'd thought then that this would make a really awesome head . . . "I'm going to build you a new body." His grin came back. "Mom always said I should try to make new friends." *And I'll make one who even gets my jokes.*

Maureen stood at the Life Sciences console with John and Don West flanking her, both men listening obediently as she began to explain her idea.

They had followed her up here without speaking a word; taken seats like two recalcitrant schoolboys, when she informed them she wasn't explaining *anything* until they explained themselves to her, and to each other . . .

She barely knew Don West, and she was no psychologist. But she was old enough to be his mother, and she'd raised three children. She'd been married to a man of few words for even longer than that. She knew by now when somebody was hurting, and afraid to admit it.

And she didn't believe Mission Control would assign them a pilot who could perform a near miracle to save them from certain death, and then nearly kill them all by his sheer recklessness.

A little gentle coaxing and her genuine concern were all it had taken to get him talking, haltingly, at last. He had looked at her the whole time, never once at John, while he told her about seeing the holograph of his best friend . . . *his only real friend* . . . who had captained the probe ship that had come to their rescue. *Five years from now.*

He told her about the spiders: what he'd seen them do, *attacking their own wounded, eating them alive*—what they must have done to the *Proteus*'s crew, and had almost done to him.

He had been staring at his hands, not even at her, when he finally admitted why he'd blown the *Proteus* to stardust.

She put out her own hand then, gently covering his, which were knotted together on the control panel; his hands felt like ice.

She looked back at John again, at last. He only shook his head, stunned into silence.

Rising from his chair, John came to her side. He put a hand on West's shoulder briefly, comfortingly. And then he put his arm around her and kissed her hair.

West looked up at them, finally, blinking too much, and for a moment his eyes seemed to be made of window glass. She saw pain and loss and confusion in that first second of contact, and then limitless depths of relief . . . He blinked again, and it was gone.

He shook his head; his face reclaimed its habitual mask of macho flyboy cool.

But at least they were finally ready to work.

"We know the atmosphere here can sustain human life." Maureen nodded at her data on the displays, wondering again whether their luck had just been phenomenally good, or whether this proved the astrophysical hypothesis that habitable planets were actually common in the galaxy. "I've located five hundred rads of radioactive material five miles west of us."

"That's at least what we'd need to get the core functioning again," John said, with actual enthusiasm in his voice. He looked out the viewport at the alien night. "We'll set off at daybreak. It'll be safer," he added, and a smile almost touched his lips as he looked back at West. "Those are my orders, Major."

West flashed him a wise-ass grin and said, "I agree with your recommendation, Professor."

Maureen folded her arms, and her smile took them both in. "Détente is a beautiful thing," she said.

In sickbay, Penny rubbed the alien baby's back gently, to keep it calm as Judy examined it. Its mottled dragon skin was warm to the touch, not rough and cold. The baby *blawp*ed contentedly, gazing up at her.

"What's the diagnosis, Doc?" Penny asked, trying for nonchalance, as if it hadn't been love at first sight for them both. "Do we go with cowboy or princess on Halloween?"

Judy looked up again. "Right now she's a girl. But I think your little pal here is from a self-replicating species . . . you know, like some kinds of lizards back on Earth. At different stages of life she, or he, probably alternates sexes."

Penny's eyebrows quirked, Groucho Marx-like. "Imagine the savings on dating outfits *alone*," she said. The tiny alien prowled the examining table as she let it go, and began to play with an aural scanner. "She sure is an interesting specimen, huh, Doc?"

"Fascinating," Judy nodded. "The retinal aperture—"

"...Can I keep her?"

"—seems linked to the digital extension—"

"*Judy?*"

"What?" Judy said impatiently, trying to finish her thought.

"Can I keep her?" Penny repeated.

Judy sighed. "Penny, she's not just another fad you can pick up and toss away." Her little sister's mind always seemed to be off in the clouds; if it wasn't for Mom, Penny would probably starve to death.

"*Please.*" Penny looked up, and Judy saw the depths of loss in her eyes. "She's all alone. I promise I'll look after her. She *needs* me."

And it was mutual...

Judy nodded finally, and took a deep breath. "The moment you *neglect* her," she began, "or forget to *feed* her . . ." She felt a flash of déjà vu. *Good grief, I'm becoming my mother.* Penny's face brightened. "Don't smile, I *mean* it, Pen—"

"Thanks, Doc!" Penny said, her smile getting even wider.

She hopped up onto the table beside the baby and began to stroke its head, as Judy started out of the room. "We're both a long way from home, aren't we, little one?" she said, in a quiet voice.

The alien looked up at her intently, and answered with a tiny *blawp*.

"That's what we'll call you," Penny declared, with sudden inspiration. "Blawp."

Blawp extended a tiny hand, touching one of the ribbons tied around Penny's arm, the red one.

"You like that?" Penny asked. She took the ribbon off and tied it around Blawp's wrist. Blawp looked up, her eyes shining with joy. Penny caressed her cheek with gentle fingers. "Nice girl," she murmured, "Pretty girl . . . Nice."

Blawp reached up to touch Penny's cheek gently in turn, chirping softly. Her tiny tongue worked as if she were trying to form the same sounds.

Standing in the hallway, Judy smiled as she watched them together, comforting each other. Her smile turned wistful and she hugged herself, feeling the chill as she went on down the hall.

Smith looked up as West entered his cell, carrying a ration pack and bedding and wearing a frown. West threw the bedding and the meal pack down on the bunk and turned to leave.

"Ah, Major," Smith said. "I see you have found a calling that suits your talents . . . Turn down the bed before you leave."

West stopped; barely controlled tension pulled him around in his tracks. "I gave my word I'd let you live," he said, the words dripping venom. "I never said for how long."

Good boy. Smith smiled faintly. *Angry at me, angry at Robinson; angry at yourself now, too?* Anger made people stupid, and West was none too bright to begin with. Only a childish, impulsive fool would have blown up the *Proteus* like he had, stranding them on this godforsaken planet. *And fools were easily led.*

Smith started across the room, putting on an expression of grim resolve. "Family hour is over, Major," he said bluntly. "We're dying here." He jerked his head at the alien night beyond the viewport.

West watched him approach; his hand went to his holstered pistol.

Smith slowed as West's face warned him off. "Robinson is out of his league," he said, holding West's gaze. "Look at his eyes. Tell me you can't see his fear—"

West made a disgusted noise, and headed for the door.

Smith leaped forward to block his path. "I fought in the millennial wars, Major!" he said, putting his back up against the door. "Survival is a soldier's game, we both know that. This civilian fool will lead us straight to hell. Robinson needs our help, whether he wants it or not! With minimal force, we could take this ship and assure this mission continues, under *your* command—"

West slapped his forehead melodramatically. "My God, Smith," he said, "you're *right*. How could I have been so blind? I'll just run and get you a *gun* so we can hijack the ship. Okay—?"

"Sarcasm is the recourse of a weak mind." Smith moved away from the door with a dismissive shrug. *All right, so West wasn't* that *stupid . . .*

"I'm hiding my pain. Really." West went out, shutting the door abruptly behind him. Smith heard the lock engage.

He waited another moment, as he had waited patiently ever since they returned from the *Proteus*; until he was sure that West would not come back. Then he reached into the cuff of his field suit, and removed the control bolt.

He had managed to take the bolt from a robot in the lockers aboard the *Proteus*, in that brief moment when West had been distracted by the ship's log Robinson had brought up on the displays. The robot that had caused him so much misery had been devoured by the spider-things—*how fitting*—but there must be others in the holds of this ship. Once he refitted the tool, he would have an unstoppable weapon at his command. And this time there would be no mistakes.

He roamed his makeshift quarters, picking up this, prying at that; auditioning various things he'd destroyed in his rage and frustration. Somewhere among them were fragments strong enough to serve as the tools he would need to retrofit the control bolt.

He *had* fought in the millennial wars. And war had taught him lessons far more valuable—far more terrible—than anyone on this ship could ever imagine.

He had been a field medic. An incompetent and corrupt commanding officer had led his entire unit into a battlefield hell-on-earth. His friends, his comrades—the ones whose wounds he'd treated and whose lives he'd tried to save, day after day—they'd all died. Everyone had died. . . . Everyone except him.

He had been the sole survivor.

Everything he valued had seemed meaningless after that . . . everything except, perversely, his own life.

Fools like the Robinsons were not fit to survive in the real universe, the one he knew. And that arrogant, incompetent excuse for a starship pilot didn't deserve to live.

It was West's fault, West's fault alone, that he was trapped here. *"I'm hiding my pain,"* West had said. West didn't know the meaning of the word. None of them did. Not yet.

"Your pain, Major West, has just begun." Smith began to resize the bolt. *There were other children on this ship; real ones. Just as there were other robots ...*

He paused a moment to scratch his back. The wound he'd gotten as they escaped from the spiders still itched and burned. *After he took control of the ship, he'd get rid of their little pet, too.*

Judy sat alone on the bridge in the pilot's chair, wrapped in a thermal blanket, sipping cold water as she stared out at the alien night. She couldn't remember the last time she had eaten, but she seemed to have no appetite for anything more. She looped a finger pensively through the strands of her uncombed hair, twined a lock around and around it. She had left her hair down because it felt warmer that way, and ... comforting, like when she was a little girl.

Someone else came onto the bridge; she turned in her seat to see Don West pause just inside the doorway. He glanced past her at the stars. "Star light, star bright ..." he recited.

She looked back at the sky. "A million strange stars,

and only one wish," she murmured, her breath frosting. "I wish we were home."

Don came and sat down in the copilot's seat, nodding as if it was his own heartfelt wish. She studied his face in profile; noticing how long his lashes were, limned by starlight. She felt the pulse begin to beat in the hollow of her throat, as it did every time she looked at him . . . as if her heart, or some other insistent part of her, had a mind of its own.

But it was a stranger's face. She looked away again at the night. "I never thought a sky could look so alien . . ." She broke off. "We really are lost."

West looked over at her, but his eyes were far away. "When the first sailors circled the globe, and saw a brand-new sky, they thought they'd sailed off the edge of the Earth," he said softly, and there was something in his voice that she had never heard before. "But they were just around the corner."

She smiled, grateful and surprised. "We just billow our sails and let the wind blow us home," she said, "is that it, Major?"

He smiled too, almost self-consciously, looking out at the stars again. "So those sailors found familiar shapes in the stars to make the skies more friendly, to help them find their way . . ." He got up and moved to the viewport. "That's how the constellations were born."

He used his finger to dot the wet film of condensation at its border with stars and connected the stars like dots in a children's book. She watched in fascination as a strangely familiar face began to take form.

"Porky," he announced, with a flourish, "the wise and mighty Pig."

She laughed in delight and stood up, moving to join him at the window. She breathed on its surface and began to draw. "The great big-eared Bunny . . . Bugs." She looked at her drawing, smiled at it. She turned to look at him, still smiling. "How you got us down here . . . that was pretty flying." Her mother had told her the rest of the story; what he'd been through, alone. She wanted to say more, but she didn't, uncertain.

Don's smile faltered, making her glad she hadn't, and then widened again as he looked into her eyes. He was standing very close to her; he leaned closer.

Judy felt her body begin to bend toward him, until her lips were almost on his; as if his very existence was a lodestone, drawing her . . .

"So, my quarters or yours?" he asked.

Judy pulled back, her mouth open in disbelief. "Excuse me?"

Don grinned, and shrugged, straightening up. "Don't play coy. We're the only single man and woman of consenting age in the galaxy. How much more of a setup do you need?"

She searched his eyes for a trace of the actual human being who had been there seconds before. But Don was gone, like a startled cat. The flyboy was back in control.

Judy leaned back against the com panel. "So you figure, just dispense with the pleasantries, get down to business—?" she said mildly.

He moved forward again, and this time she had to

control the urge to step away. "You have a way with words, Doctor."

She smiled seductively. "You gonna show me how you handle the helm . . . ?"

His grin widened. ". . . Yeah," he said.

She bent her head as she ran a hand along the control panel, letting her hair slide down across her shoulder, and her smile reel him in. "Right here? On this console?"

His face was right up to hers now, their lips only a breath apart. "Oh, here would be fine," he whispered. He closed his eyes; his lips—*oh, such kissable lips*—parted for her kiss.

Her hand closed around her water glass. She inverted it over his head. *Instant cold shower.*

Don gasped; his eyes opened wide and the water sluiced down his face, blinding him.

As he rubbed his vision clear, she held up the empty glass. "You just hang on to your joystick . . ." she said, and tapped his dripping nose. Rising from her seat, she winked at him before she walked away.

"Excellent technique, Major," he muttered to himself, mopping his sodden brow. "Really."

John activated the automated security systems, and crossed the room to his wife. Maureen sat on the edge of their bed in her thermals, brushing her hair—getting ready for their first night's sleep on another world. *Long* couldn't begin to describe this day, he thought numbly; but then, the words that could describe it probably hadn't been invented yet.

"Will was looking for you," Maureen said.

He nodded, overwhelmed by fatigue as he sat down beside her. "I sent him to bed." He rubbed his eyes, his aching head. "Now he's decided he can rebuild the robot. Wants to stay up all night and show me his designs . . ." He sighed, wishing Will was old enough to get his priorities straight.

Maureen put her brush away. "Funny creatures, men," she said, her voice getting that tone she had. "You try so hard not to be your fathers . . . and end up making the same mistakes."

The words were like a rifle shot, causing everything about this terrible day to come avalanching down on him. "We can't get off this planet, much less back on course!" he said angrily. "I don't have time to—" He broke off.

Maureen looked away, as if she was biting her tongue to keep from snapping back at him. When she finally looked at him again, he saw apology in her eyes. She raised her hand and began gently massaging his neck. "John, just listen to him . . ." she said. "It doesn't matter what he's saying. Just *listen*. Sometimes, at least in the eyes of their fathers, little boys have to come first."

John put his arm around her, holding her close. He knew as well as she did that her words about his father stung because they were true. *He had always sworn that he wouldn't be that way; he would put his family first, and keep his promises*. It was why they had come on this journey together. "As soon as we get back into space," he murmured, "we're going to spend some real time together. I promise."

Maureen stared out the viewport; she didn't answer. He felt her body droop as she sat looking out at the night, as if he hadn't even spoken. He held her closer, telling himself that she was just too tired to understand, or he was . . .

After a moment she looked back at him again, and smiled.

"What?" John asked, perplexed.

Her smile widened ruefully. "It's nice to have our family under one roof. Even if we had to go halfway across the galaxy to manage it . . ."

Alone on the bridge, Don put the ship to bed; closing the blast shields that shuttered the ports, shutting down redundant systems, ordering the com to sleep. He started out of the room, heading for his own quarters, where he was going to be sleeping alone.

As he walked along the dim and silent corridor, he heard Maureen Robinson say, "Good night, John," and her husband answer, "Good night, Maureen."

He took three more strides.

"Good night, Judy," Will called.

"Good night, Will," Penny answered.

"Good night, Penny," Judy said.

West stopped in his tracks, shaking his head. "You guys have *got* to be kidding!" he said loudly. He walked on.

"*Blawp*," said Blawp.

Chapter Seventeen

Will Robinson sat in his father's com chair, rubbing his eyes. He was the first one awake, and he felt like his mind had been thinking up new ideas for his robot-building project all the while he slept. He couldn't wait to start implementing them. *And nobody else was awake to tell him he couldn't.*

The smarting memory of his father's latest rejection faded as he began to wake up the ship. The main monitor read SOLAR BATTERIES RECHARGED. *Cool.* He could use all the power he wanted, without anybody getting mad. He thumbed a button to open the blast shields, eager for his first real daylight look at the new planet.

He leaned forward, blinking as sunlight streamed in over the displays. As he got his first clear view of the outside, his eyes widened in disbelief.

About a hundred meters out from the ship, shimmering hypnotically on the bleak snowy shore, was a flame-ringed portal exactly like the one they had entered yesterday, up in space. But beyond the threshold of this one he could see a summer day, and a world filled with strange crayon-bright plant life.

Will leaped from his seat and went running out of the

room, yelling, "Mom! Dad!" It was definitely time for everybody to wake up.

His wake-up call achieved its purpose with stunning speed, for once. It wasn't every morning your family woke up to an interdimensional portal, instead of cereal and juice.

They all gathered in the dayroom, yawning and fastening their flight suits, for a breakfast of field rations washed down with water. No one complained, though; they were too busy staring at the portal on the display screens.

Judy sat down across the table. Don West came in and sat beside her. Will watched Don pointedly move her water glass as far away as possible. Judy let him, smiling like the Cheshire Cat.

Will wondered what *that* was about.

A deep rumbling rolled through the ground beneath the ship; even the air seemed to vibrate, distracting him from his sister's weirdness. He'd felt the first tremor just after he woke up, and there had been more since. It seemed odd that they hadn't felt any yesterday.

"Okay," his father said, "let's get settled. Maureen?"

Mom stood up and put her data on the big screen.

It was a geological map of the planet's surface that she'd had the computer put together for them. But he'd never seen one like this before. It was totally bizarro . . . like a jigsaw puzzle put together by a gorilla.

"It's impossible," Mom said, pointing at the screen as she spoke his thoughts out loud, "but this planet's continental plates don't match up."

"I was afraid of this," Dad muttered. Everyone turned to stare at him. He glanced up at them, then looked down at the floor, gesturing. "I think these tremors are the result of opening and closing doorways."

"Doorways to where?" Penny asked. Her alien, Blawp, sat in her lap, peering over the table's edge. It was cute, but Will was glad he had the Robot.

"The future," Dad said.

Major West made a noise like a cat's sneeze. "Perhaps the Professor was hit on the head when we landed," he said sarcastically.

What a dork. Will frowned at him. So did Judy.

Dad looked at Don the way he always looked at Will when he was trying to be patient. "Think about it," he said, looking at Don again before he went on speaking to them all. "The portal that led us to the probe ship. The advanced technology they used to track us through hyperspace. Don's friend, looking so old . . ." His glance flickered back to West. "What if we crossed into a time years after Earth sent a rescue mission?"

"You're not serious?" Don said. But he didn't sound so sure this time. "Time travel is impossible—"

"No it's not!" Will interrupted impatiently. "It's just improbable. Like hyperdrive was a hundred years ago. Nothing's *really* impossible." He shrugged.

His father nodded, not even glancing at him. "This world could be riddled with doorways to the future."

"So if we walk into that forest outside," Will pointed toward the viewport, "we're really just walking into this crater, years from now."

"Geological plates from different times wouldn't fit

together," Mom said, smiling her approval at him. "That would explain the continental mismatch. But, doorways in time . . . ?" She looked back at Dad.

Dad shrugged. "It's hard for me to believe, too," he said to her. "But if these portals *are* opening and closing, part of some cascading natural phenomenon, they could be tearing this planet apart."

Will felt the wild lightning of inspiration strike his brain. "What if the doorways *aren't* natural—?"

"Will," Dad glanced at him as if *he* was being a dork, "this kind of phenomenon could only be produced naturally."

"No—" Will insisted, feeling his frustration rise with his excitement. "These portals are exactly what I predicted my time machine would do! What if someone on this world has built a device—"

Dad silenced him with a look. "Son, I appreciate your input, but now isn't the time for flights of fancy."

Will started up out of his seat. "You *never* listen to me!" he shouted at his father. "Not *ever*." He ran out of the room.

John didn't move from the head of the table as Will stormed out of the dayroom. Maureen watched her husband struggling to make the right choice, torn between love and duty. Duty won, again. But in his eyes she saw the pain of defeat, and it made her heart ache.

"There's no telling how long before this planet breaks up entirely." John stood up, addressing the others as if there had been no interruption. "The Major and I are going to locate the radioactive material for the core. We may have very little time." He nodded at West, a signal that they should get going, and headed for the door.

Will looked up from tinkering with his deck as his father entered the robot bay.

"I'm leaving now, Will," Dad said.

"*That's* a surprise," Will said sullenly. Dad was already all suited up for the mission, like he couldn't wait to be gone.

His father came on across the room, and stood looking down at him. "Will, you're the most important thing in the world to me," Dad said softly. "I hope one day you'll be able to see that."

Will looked away, biting his lip, as tears suddenly welled up inside him. "What if one time you don't come home . . . ?" he said at last, his voice squeaking.

Dad gazed down at him as if he didn't know how to answer, and Will saw his own fear reflected in his father's eyes. Finally his father reached up, and took off the dog tags he always wore. "Whenever your grandfather went away on a mission," he said, "he'd leave these with me. For safekeeping. And when he got home, I'd always be waiting to give them back."

Dad hung the chain carefully around Will's neck; the dog tags clinked against his chest. "I'm coming back, Will," Dad said, his voice straining. "I *promise*."

Will looked up at him, wide-eyed, silent. His father ruffled his hair gently, then turned and left the room. Will looked down again, fingering the tags. He knew the story of how his grandfather had left them with Dad, always promising him the same thing. . . . He knew about the last time, when Grandpa didn't come back.

Don started, as if he'd been lost in thought, when Judy joined him outside the ship's main hatch. He was dressed in thermal expedition gear, and a pulse rifle rested against the icicle-hung landing strut beside him. She supposed he must have been expecting her father.

His face came alive as he saw her; but then his smile faltered. "Listen," he mumbled, looking down at the ground, "about last night . . ."

Come on, flyboy— She smiled, but he didn't see it. "Go ahead," she said encouragingly, "you can do it."

Don lifted his head, looking embarrassed and hopeful and pained all at once. "I'm sorry . . . ?"

Yes! she thought. *Yes, yes, yes!* "See. That wasn't so difficult."

Don grimaced. "Like pulling steel needles through my cheeks," he said, with a reluctant smile.

She nodded wryly. "Then you'll understand what saying *this* feels like." Moving closer, she looked up into his eyes. "Try to come back in one piece . . ." She folded her hands shut over the urge to reach out and touch him.

He beamed, and edged a little closer. "I'm thinking this is your basic kiss-for-luck occasion . . . wouldn't you agree, Doc?"

She looked at him. "*Thinking.*" She tapped her forehead. "Not really your strong suit . . ." She smiled then,

in all seriousness, and said, "Kisses have to be earned."
Like respect.

He looked at her. Went on looking at her, this time, in a completely new way . . . letting her into his eyes, welcoming her into his thoughts. He nodded once, his own mouth turning up in a quirky smile.

Her father emerged from the ship, and then the rest of the family . . . all except Will, she noticed. Don slung his rifle at his back, barely taking his eyes off her as he did, smiling all the while.

Her mother handed her father a small tracking device. "I've got a fix on the radioactive material. It's through the portal."

Dad nodded. "We'll just have to hope the doorways remain stable." He glanced toward the portal shimmering like blown silk a short walk away across the stony, snow-dappled ground. The golden summer day beyond it seemed to be beckoning them to step through the looking glass . . .

Judy looked back at her father, at Don, trying to keep the anxiety she felt off of her face. It made sense that they should go; they were the ones with military training. But—

"These crater walls are disabling the comm links." Mom nodded at the icy, rust-red cliff face, as calmly as if she was telling Dad to call if he'd be late for dinner. "You won't be able to communicate with the ship."

The ground trembled beneath their feet; rumbling filled the air and faded away, as if they were being warned that time was short.

Mom reached up suddenly to touch Dad's face. "Come home to me, Professor . . ."

"I love you, wife," he murmured, smiling into her eyes.

Blawp reached up from Penny's shoulder at her urging, patting Dad's face in imitation of Mom's gesture. *"Nice girl,"* she chirped. *"Pretty girl. Nice."*

Judy stared in surprise as Penny stroked Blawp's head, beaming proudly. She looked back at Don again as her father picked up his rifle and started toward the portal. Don fell in beside him, looking over his shoulder at her . . . at her family . . . as if he were taking a mental picture of them. As if, no matter what happened, he wanted to carry this moment with him always.

John reached the portal first, and stood staring at it. He put out a hand, passing it through the gate's rippling, illusory surface. He felt nothing more than a faint tingling as his hand distorted eerily. "Wow," he murmured softly, drawing it back again.

"Oh," West said, coming up beside him. *"That's* scientific."

John glanced over at him, too full of wonder at what they were about to experience even to feel annoyed. As West looked at the portal, John saw something come into the younger man's eyes that he had never expected to see there: West was staring at the portal as if he were facing the guillotine.

Defending the hypergate against enemy raiders, or diving through the sun, he was fearless; because piloting a ship was what he did, and he knew what the odds were, he understood all the rules. But he wasn't a scientist.

John felt his own heart racing; but it was anticipation he felt—excitement, awe—because he was about to experience something beyond a physicist's wildest dreams. This was his final frontier . . . He couldn't wait to step through into the Unknown.

"Scared, Major?" he said, with a sudden grin.

And then he took the first step.

Don sucked in his breath as Robinson stepped through the portal; as his image distorted, whipping away into the future like blown smoke. Don froze, gazing through the window of time; until suddenly he saw Robinson on the other side, looking back at him from inside the summer day. He shook his head in amazement. And then he shut his eyes. And followed.

Chapter
Eighteen

Will kneeled on the floor of the robot bay, picking through the personal cargo containers he'd packed only two days ago. He glanced up at the Robot's partially assembled body sitting on the work table, considered the possibilities of the toy he was holding, and then set it aside.

Penny came into the room, carrying an assortment of hair clips and other metal and electronic objects. She dumped them on the table. She had actually *volunteered* to help him, when she found out what he was doing. Maybe that little alien monkey had telepathic powers or something; she was a lot nicer in general now that she had it.

"That's everything even close to nonessential," Penny announced. "Even my belly-button ring."

"Thanks, Pen," he said, smiling.

She came over to look down at him and his bin of belongings. "You want to come outside?"

He shook his head, his smile disappearing. He hadn't left the robot bay since his father had stopped in to say good-bye. He didn't want to; this was the only place where anybody really needed him. The Robot *needed* him.

"Look, what does Dad know?" Penny said softly. "Maybe someone *did* build a time machine." She ruffled his hair with her hand, the way Dad would have, and went out of the room.

Will got up with a querulous sigh, and crossed to the console. "Can you hear me, Robot?" he asked.

"*Robot is on line,*" it answered. "*Your voice modulation is peculiar. Is something wrong, Will Robinson?*"

Will choked on the emotions caught in his throat, and didn't say anything.

"*Cheer up,*" the Robot said heartily, when he didn't answer. "*I will tell you a joke. Why did the Robot cross the road?*" It waited a beat for him to respond, and then it said, "*Because he was carbon-bonded to the chicken!*" The Robot laughed, loudly.

Will rolled his eyes. "*We've* got some work to do...." he said.

As he began to turn away again, a knocking sound echoed faintly through the wall of the bay. He listened, puzzled.

"*It sounds like old Morse code,*" the Robot commented.

"What's it say?" he asked.

"'*Danger, Will Robinson. Danger,*'" the Robot said.

Will went out of the bay and walked along the corridor, tracing the knocking back to its source.

Its source was the room where Doctor Smith was being held. Will peered in through the window in the door. Smith sat at a table, hammering out the code with his boot. He looked up as if he sensed Will's presence, and stopped banging to beckon him inside.

Will hesitated. Then he took a laser pistol from its mount on the wall, voice-coded it to respond only to him, and opened the door.

"You said someone is in danger." He stood warily, holding the gun where Smith could see it.

Smith's eyes went to the weapon like BBs to a magnet. "We all are. You are wise to arm yourself." He got up from the table, approaching Will.

"This gun is set to fire for me only, so don't try anything funny," Will said sharply.

Smith shrugged and passed on by, only going to the viewport to open its blast shield. "William, you misjudge me," he said. "I only want to help you."

"*Help* us?" Will said increduously. "You tried to *kill* us."

Smith sighed in annoyance as he turned back to face Will. "But now our fates are intertwined," he pointed out, and Will realized that was true. "If your father and that idiot West fail, I will have no chance of getting home. It is in my best interests that they succeed. And I always follow my best interests." He looked back out the window, at the strange landscape and stranger flora lying beyond the portal. Somewhere out there, something gave an inhuman wail that made Will's skin prickle.

Smith looked back at him again, as if the sound only proved his point. "What monsters roam these alien wilds—?" He waved his hand at the viewport. "Those fools. To set off blindly across this savage land . . . Much as I hate to admit it, it *will* be harder to manage without them."

Will shifted nervously. "What are you talking about?" he demanded. "They'll be back. They'll be okay." Suddenly he was not sure whether he was trying to convince Smith, or himself.

Smith stared darkly at him. "Will they?" he asked.

Will bit his lip, feeling worry and fear churn in the pit of his stomach. He glanced at the window, seeing the portal's eerie shimmer against the divided sky. "Someone should go after them . . ."

"Will, I forbid it," Smith said sternly. He shook his head. "You're a boy. A clever one, certainly, but a child nonetheless. This planet is likely full of predators. Even if you found them, what if they're hurt, ravaged, dying . . . what good could *you* do—?"

Will's face furrowed. *Too little; he was always too little to help!* And the Robot's body wasn't finished. "But you're a doctor," he said, with sudden inspiration. Smith *needed* them, to survive; he'd said so himself. Smith had to help him.

Smith turned away to the window, his hands clasped behind him. "Yes," he murmured thoughtfully. "Yes, I am . . ."

Penny braced her feet against the ship's outer hull, hanging from a rapelling line alongside her sister and her mother as they spot-welded and sealed the damage their crash-landing had done.

"I need a microsealer," Mom said, pushing her goggles up on her forehead. She gestured at a puncture wound where entrails of cable and flexible conduit spilled out through the ship's charred designation logo, dangling in the air.

Penny flipped the release on her harness and sailed down the rope to the ground. This was one job she loved; fetching tools was like mountaineering.

Rooting through a tool kit, she noticed her cam/watch lying where she had left it for safekeeping. She looked at it thoughtfully, then activated it and said, "After much deliberation, the Space Captive has decided to accept her new role as a member of the crew. The Robinsons, after all, can obviously *use* her help . . ."

She broke off her narration as she realized that Blawp was no longer investigating tool boxes and playing with pebbles anywhere around her.

She stood up, her gaze sweeping a wider and wider area until she was looking at the portal. And Blawp, who was crouched at its edge, sniffing curiously.

"Blawp!" she called. "Blawp, come away from there—"

Blawp looked up, as if she was about to come racing back at Penny's call. But then she looked through at the strange forest beckoning from the other side.

And stepped into it.

"Blawp!" Penny scrambled up, dropping her cam/watch as she ran toward the portal. "Wait—!"

Will led Doctor Smith through the russet moss-forest into a field of flowers like no flowers he had ever seen, their lushly blue-violet petals moving in the breeze like an indigo sea. "Wow, that's Mom's favorite color—"

"How droll," Smith commented wearily, behind him.

Will looked back, half frowning. He wished he could show Mom the flowers; wished even more that she was *here* with him. But they'd sneaked out of the ship without telling anyone, at Smith's urging. Smith said his mother would try to stop them, and that nagging little voice in the back of his mind had agreed: She would say this was wrong; it wasn't safe for him to go; he was too little ... *Even Mom wouldn't understand.*

He looked down at the tracking device he carried in his hand. It still showed them on a course toward the radioactive material Dad had gone after. Since he hadn't been there to tell Dad good-bye, he hadn't seen which direction his father and Major West set off in, once they went through the portal. Finding them was a lot harder than he'd expected.

Another earth tremor bore down on them, stronger than any before, approaching with terrifying speed. Smith gasped suddenly. Will turned and saw the very air in the distance begin to warp into swirling distortion, like water being sucked down a drain. Inside it, flowers bloomed and died within seconds, trees rose and fell, as the twisted, billowing landscape aged years with every heartbeat.

"Run, child, run!" Smith shouted, grabbing Will's arm and jerking him forward. They ran. But there was no way anything alive could outrun that tornado of time bearing down on them—

Doctor Smith stumbled suddenly and pitched headlong into the flowers, dragging Will down with him.

* * *

Smith's misstep landed him facedown in a miasma of damp earth and crushed petals. He barely noticed, as the roaring and shaking filled all his senses. He shut his eyes, clutching the broken plant stems in a death grip as he waited for the inevitable to strike him down ...

After another interminable moment, he opened his eyes again. He raised his head and turned, slowly, to look back.

The glowing portal had stopped, inexplicably, ten meters short of sucking them into an early grave.

Beyond the portal lay a newly stabilized landscape, a landscape far older, darker, and more overgrown than the one in which he lay. *Oh, Dorothy,* he thought, *we're really not in Kansas anymore.* He realized suddenly that Will was nowhere in sight.

"Will?" he shouted. "Will!" The boy had been right beside him. Surely he hadn't been—

Will's head sprouted abruptly from among the leaves. "Cool . . ." he breathed as he looked beyond Smith, eyes shining. He scrambled to his feet and darted toward the new portal. He stopped barely short of it, peering through into the other reality. And then he crossed over into it.

"William, wait!" Smith shouted, too late.

Will waved at him from the other side, grinning. "It's just like stepping between rooms!" he called.

"I can barely contain my glee." Smith grimaced, getting painfully to his feet.

Will glanced down at his tracker again, and looked off into the distance. "Dad's signal is this way!" he cried, pointing into the stygian woods. "Come on, Doctor

Smith—" He set off into the underbrush without even a backward glance.

Smith stood staring after him. "I *loathe* children," he said to the air. They existed for only one purpose, in his mind: as bargaining chips. Who was it who'd said, "He who has children gives hostages to Fortune". . . ? It hardly mattered. All that mattered now was catching up with the others. Once West was out of the way, Robinson would do anything he was told, to protect his son . . . He took a deep breath and started for the portal.

This passage deeper into time was neither as unpleasant nor as disorienting as he had feared. He entered the dank, loathsomely overgrown forest, pushing himself to catch up with the over-eager Robinson boy. He kept fit, but even in his youth he'd never had the kind of hyperactive energy this child seemed to have.

The plant life of this world was almost fungoidal; touching it was as repulsive as touching moldy bread. He stumbled over something in the underbrush beside a turbid stream; looked down, watching his steps more carefully.

As he started on, something in the undergrowth caught his eye—something manmade. A flattened scrap of metal. He stopped, pushing away the foliage until the unnatural shapes stood revealed. His frown deepened.

Will reappeared suddenly, up ahead between the trees. "What did you find?" he asked.

Smith let the foliage fall back into place and hurried forward, catching Will by the shoulders as he tried to get past for a look. "Come, come, son, no time to dawdle," he said briskly. "Let's move along." He nudged

Will, propelling him on into the forest before he could see the grave markers. Three of them. Bearing the names of Maureen, Penny, and Judy Robinson.

"Blawp? Blawp—!" Penny pushed through the amber moss forest on the other side of the portal, frantic with worry. *How was she ever going to find her in all this—?*

Suddenly she heard a faint, familiar *blawp*ing from somewhere up ahead. She ran forward, tracking the sound through the dwinding undergrowth until a red rock cliff rose up in her path, its time-etched face a bizarre wonderland of overhangs and caverns. And there was Blawp, in an open space among the moss-draped spires, hopping up and down, *chirp*ing and *blawp*ing. Penny couldn't see anything for her to be *blawp*ing at.

Maybe she was just frightened because she was lost. "Blawp," she scolded, coming forward, "you can't run *off* like that!"

Blawp began to shriek hysterically as something thudded down between them, engulfing Penny in a smokescreen of dust. Penny skidded to a halt, coughing and waving the dust out of her face. As it cleared she saw something *huge* begin to appear, seemingly from nowhere, within the cloud.

Her mouth fell open as she saw it clearly: It was some kind of alien, standing nearly twice her height. Its massive arms and the hump of its alligator-hided back bristled with spines; the blunt tip of its tail was studded with spikes, like a mace. It had a face like an orangutan, and bulging binocular eyes.

She stood gaping, wanting to feel afraid. But before her stunned brain could move beyond shock into fear, she saw the faded, tattered red ribbon tied around its finger . . .

Blawp saw the ribbon at the same moment. She launched herself at the big alien, shrieking in rage.

"Blawp, *no!*" Penny cried, lunging forward to grab her, too late.

Blawp vaulted into the air and landed on the creature's enormous arm; she caught the frayed end of the ribbon, tugging at it with furious jealousy.

Penny stared, her amazement growing, as the giant did not shrug Blawp off like a fly, but only stood gazing down at her . . . *tenderly?*

Blawp gave up her frenzied attack as the alien did nothing to try and stop her. She settled back in the crook of the creature's arm, peering up at its face in curiosity. Then she looked at the ribbon around her wrist, at the ribbon on its finger, back and forth — realizing what Penny had already seen: that the two ribbons, except for their age, were exactly the same one.

Slowly, the alien giant came toward Penny, step by step. Penny stood where she was, paralyzed by the conflicting urges to stay and to run away, as it raised an enormous paw, reaching toward her. With amazing gentleness, it touched her cheek. "Nice girl," it said. "Pretty girl. Nice."

Penny gazed up into its face, her eyes filling with tears of wonder. *This was going to make* such *an awesome story . . .*

✻   ✻   ✻

John and Don West passed through another portal, following the tracker's lead toward the still-elusive fuel source. Each new reality they entered seemed bleaker than the last, even as it took them further and further from safety, and away from the people who were depending on their success.

And yet with every passage through another time-gate, John felt his thoughts growing clearer, his mind coming more alive. "Extraordinary. I think each portal we cross moves us further in time." *Only into the future. Never into the past . . . Why?* And if it was time they were traversing, not space, they could even be walking in circles, paradoxically crossing the same stretch of terrain over and over as it aged . . .

Paradox was what time travel was all about—or so the theories had it. All the theory he'd ever studied suddenly seemed as simplistic as a stick-figure drawing, compared with his present reality.

"Fantastic," West muttered, hunching his shoulders and shifting from foot to foot as he gazed out at the rust-colored badlands.

John looked back at the gate shimmering in the air behind them. "Imagine an energy field that could manipulate space-time singularities to produce these kinds of localized vortex effects!" He shook his head in amazement as cascading insights went off like fireworks inside his brain. He hadn't felt a pure, ecstatic sense of wonder like this since he was a boy, working on his hyperspace theorem. "Wow! Both Einstein and Tagamishi speculated that at a quantum or even sub-quantum level . . ." He glanced back at West.

West was staring at him, with a look he knew all too well: the same look of incomprehension and exasperation that everyone he'd known as a boy, including his own parents, had worn, whenever he'd tried to share the amazing world inside his mind with them.

John looked down, and away, shrugging.

They began to walk again, entering an arid plain dotted with hairy, trilobed plant life. The amber hummocks reminded him of cactus.

"That would be one great climb," West said after a time, finally breaking the awkward silence they'd kept until then. He gestured toward the red, eroded rock face they were approaching. In the younger man's eyes— John saw the echo of all the risk-taking adrenaline highs West had ever known—the moments he lived for, the moments when he had proved to Death that he was fully, completely alive. *Because life was not a dress rehearsal; mistakes or not, this was all the chance you ever got to make memories worth looking back on.*

John suddenly remembered his father, in a way he hadn't for years: *how his father had taken him rock-climbing, hiking, skiing, in the wilderness preserve near their home. Not out of duty, or because the Old Man wanted to toughen up his tech-nerd son, but because it was exciting, because it was fun. Because he'd loved it there, in that dwindling refuge of Earth's beauty. They both had.* "You know," he said, smiling a little, "my father would have liked you."

West looked startled; his sudden grin filled with pleasure and pride.

It was close to sundown by the time they finally

reached the cliff face. John checked the tracking device again. "*Damn.*"

"Damn?" West echoed, half frowning. "Damn is not good."

"I am a *fool,*" John said furiously, looking up. This was the sourcepoint of the signal. But there was nothing here. Only a stone wall; a dead end. "The signal we've been tracking is the *Jupiter's* core material, reflecting off these rocks—" He turned, looking back the way they had come.

As he moved, a flash of unexpected light speared his eye from ground level. He looked down.

He was standing on a slab of metal covered with red dirt.

He stepped back. West hauled the piece of wreckage upright, grimacing with the effort, and brushed it off with his hand.

On it, still clearly readable, was the logo of the *Jupiter Two.*

John swore softly. "This metal is decades old . . ." He ran his hand over its patinaed surface.

West let go of the metal plate as if it were burning hot; it thudded in the dust at his feet. "What kind of nightmare *is* this?" His eyes raked the alien landscape, came back to John's face with a kind of desperation. "Where the hell are we—?"

"No, Major. . . ." John shook his head. He'd been right, in his feeling that they were traveling in circles. "The question is, *when* the hell are we?"

The superheated air *crack*ed open as an energy bolt caught West in the back, punching him across the open space onto his face.

John hit the ground and rolled to cover behind an outcrop of stone. He unslung his rifle and began to return fire. More explosive bursts blasted the rocks in front of him. He ducked; pushed up again to fire off another round of shots —

The lash of energy caught him from behind, just like West, and swatted him down into blackness.

The two men lay still in the dirt.

The Robot rolled out from among the rocks, its makeshift body scarred by the passage of long, hard years. It raised its arms, its pincer claws extended.

Will and Doctor Smith continued their journey through the bleak, unpromising land beyond another portal, still following the tracker's signal. They had long ago left the brooding jungle behind, for a red-rock desert where the eroded soil looked like tire treads. The two suns hung low in the crimson sky, casting long sinuous shadows with blurred edges like a double exposure.

Now they were working their way down a slope through a maze of hairy, bulbous cactuses. Some of the plants were as tall as he was; they made him feel as if he were trapped in a herd of lemmings, being carried along toward some unknown disaster.

The strangeness had stopped seeming cool to him hours ago; now it was even past scary and depressing. He wanted to be back with his family so much that he had actually begun to feel that something about this creepy landscape looked familiar . . .

"I feel like we got turned around," he said unhappily.

"Just follow your father's signal, young William," Smith repeated, with strained patience.

Will looked down at the tracker again, and off in the direction it was indicating. "Oh, shit," he whispered.

"A boy of your intelligence shouldn't swear," Smith said disapprovingly.

Will pointed straight ahead. "Look."

Smith looked up, following his gesture. "Oh," he said at last. "Shit, indeed."

Ahead of them in the distance, glowing like a beacon fire in the last light of the setting suns, was the *Jupiter Two*. It sat below the same wall of red stone, lodged up against the crater's rim . . . but not the way he remembered it.

This *Jupiter Two* had been gutted. Its lower sections were gone; the scarred hull lay open to the sky, its metal peeled back like a broken tin can. *Mom. Penny. Judy—* With a cry he began to run down the slope.

Chapter Nineteen

John stirred as consciousness brought him back, reluctantly, into his body. His mind replayed its final memory inside his eyelids as he tried to raise his head: *Ambushed. Shot. But still alive . . .*

He was inside a structure of some sort; one that must have survived some terrible disaster. The vast space was mostly dark, mostly in shadow; in a few isolated spots lamps burned, and the last light of day still penetrated through gaping rents in its walls. It was clearly high tech—computer consoles, control panels, screens—but most of the tech looked long dead. Here and there a few functional displays flickered, monitoring some system's failing heartbeat.

He was lying in an empty corner of the room, as if he'd been dropped there like trash. He rolled over and found West beside him, singed and battered, still unconscious. *But alive, thank God . . .* He wondered morbidly whether he looked that bad. He felt that bad.

"Well, well . . ." a man's voice said, echoing from broken surfaces. "All things really do come to he who waits."

John struggled to sit up, using the wall at his back for

support. A lone figure was sitting across the room, his face obscured by shadow. "What is this place?" John asked.

"The shock must have scrambled your brain," the stranger said sardonically. "Look around. Don't you recognize the spot? You're home."

Home? John stared at the shadow figure. "This can't be . . ." *Oh, God. It was. The* Jupiter Two.

"What have you done to the ship?" He pushed to his feet, the pain it cost him to stand lost inside his sudden, terrible fear. "*Where's my family?*"

"Your family is dead," the man said. "Dead and in the ground."

"*No—*" John whispered, feeling the bottom drop out of his soul.

The man in the shadows stood, rising into the light so that John could see his face. He was nearly John's age; his clothing was dirty and worn, his blond hair and beard were long and unkempt. He looked like a hermit just emerging from a cave. *And yet, they could have been brothers* . . .

"I'll never forget that morning," the stranger said, "twenty, thirty years ago? What was it you said: 'I'll be back. I promise.' But I knew better . . . *You never came home.*"

He moved slowly across the room to one of the burned-out panels. "Without you, your family never had a chance. A few spiders survived the destruction of the probe ship. They reached the planet and attacked. I can still hear the women scream . . ."

"Who *are* you?" John asked hoarsely.

The stranger came toward him then, stopped inside a circle of lamplight. His hand rose to something dangling against his chest, and he held it out. "Don't you recognize me, Dad?" Tarnished metal winked in the light: *Dog tags.* "I'm your son, Will."

"Penny? Penny—"

Penny looked up as her mother and Judy burst out of the brush and into the cavernous space where she sat cross-legged with the two Blawps. She grinned.

They stopped, laser pistols in hand, and stared at the enormous creature gently touching Penny's face.

"*Penny?*" Mom gasped. "Baby, are you all right?"

Penny nodded, getting to her feet. "It's okay, Mom," she said briskly, waving at them to put their guns away. "She's not going to hurt us. It's like she thinks I'm her princess or something . . ."

She wondered how they'd ever managed to find her here, until she remembered her cam/watch . . . they must have heard her calling Blawp. She went forward to meet them, carrying Blawp in her arms. The giant alien hung back, its strange face filled with awe and reverence.

Her mother and Judy came forward almost as shyly as the alien did, as she introduced them to each other. But the alien accepted them calmly, letting Judy examine her almost as if she remembered everything that had happened yesterday . . . or years ago.

"Best as I can tell," Judy murmured, turning back to face them, "this creature is pregnant. But . . ." She held up her hands.

"Speak, Doctor," Mom said.

Judy made a dubious face. "All life forms have unique biopatterns. As individual as fingerprints, no two alike. Except . . ."

"Except the biopatterns of this giant creature and our little Blawp match exactly. Don't they?" Mom finished, looking at the two aliens with a strange expression on her face.

Judy stared at her. "How did you know?"

Mom's gaze glanced off the time-eaten surface of the crater wall, and back at Blawp sitting in Penny's lap. "Because, I think Blawp and our friend here are actually one and the same."

Well, duh, Penny thought. Her family would figure things out *so* much faster if they'd just learn to trust their instincts. But at least they *did* figure things out. . . . She smiled, looking proudly at them all. *This is going to make the awesomest story* ever.

The Robot shoved John forward roughly, carrying West's unconscious body slung over its other arm as Will lead them along the empty corridors to the *Jupiter's* gutted engine room.

"Father, I give you . . . eternity." Will gestured toward what had once been the hyperdrive initiator. John stumbled to a halt in the center of the room, staring at what had become of it, and back at what had become of his son . . . feeling the converging courses of reality and nightmare finally merge.

A glowing energy bubble hung suspended beneath

the hyperdrive initiator, hovering over its shattered basin. Within the bubble incoherent images swirled, almost but never quite coalescing into something recognizable.

Eternity...? John realized that he was looking at eternity: that the device was some sort of permutation on the time portals that had led him here. Had Will somehow found a way to control the forces behind them?

The Robot dropped West unceremoniously in a heap. The impact jarred him awake; he rolled over, groaning. "Where are we?" he said thickly, holding his head as John helped him sit up.

John glanced away at Will. "I think we've come back to the *Jupiter* decades after we left," he murmured.

"*Look,* Father, what my 'flights of fancy' have created!" Will demanded, refusing to let John's attention leave him again. "I used your hyperengine to build my time machine!"

West's mouth opened as the grown man across the room called John "Father." After a second he swore softly, as if he had assembled all the impossible fragments, and seen what kind of picture they made.

Will crossed the room to what had once been John's chair at the com. The console sat at the center of a massive tangle of cables, its cybernetic circuitry linking the hyperengine and something on the upper gantry like the webwork of an insane spider. "Over the years, I have struggled to harness the awesome power of time. All my experiments at creating a stable doorway have failed. Until now." He touched a button on the console, and somewhere a generator came on, illuminating an active fuel cylinder from the starship's original drive unit.

"The core material," West whispered. The dazed slur was gone from his voice, and his eyes were clear. "If we could get that back to our *Jupiter Two* . . ."

John nodded, never taking his eyes off his son. Creating a stable doorway . . . *My God*, he thought. *Will hadn't contained a natural phenomenon—he'd caused it.* Will's time machine had created the unstable portals, not the other way around . . . and they were tearing this planet apart.

"Once this core material is fully introduced into the control console," Will said, his voice rising, "I will open a doorway stable enough for one person to take one trip through time and space as well. Today, I will change history—!" Will input another command, and John watched the energy bubble drift down through the air, until it disappeared into the hyperengine basin waiting below. A monitor came alive, showing him an image of the Earth.

"*I* will return home," Will said, his eyes burning, "to the day you took us on this cursed mission. I'll stop us from taking off. I'll do what *you* never could! *I'll save the family.* I'll save us all!" His voice trembled.

John choked on grief as he watched his son, and listened to him speak. *God, Will was insane . . . the years alone had driven him mad.* He had failed Will—failed everyone he loved—and his failure was a thousand times more terrible than anything he'd ever blamed his own father for.

He shook his head, shaking loose his thoughts. "Will,

look around—" He waved his hand. "The force of your time machine is ripping this planet apart! What if it has the same effect on Earth? What if, in getting home, you destroy Earth in the process?"

Will turned his back and started to walk away, heading for the console. "I'm going home," he repeated. "I'm going to save the family."

"Will, I'm your father!" John said desperately. "You've got to listen to me—!"

Will spun around, his face a mask of hatred. "Let me tell you about *my father*," he said. "*My father* was a walking ghost. He dragged his family into deep dark space and *lost* them there. *My father* is not coming to the rescue!" He went to the console beside the coalescing space-time wormhole without looking back again.

Don got slowly to his feet, his expression a gridlock of emotions. He stared at John, back at the forty-year-old man who was John's son, and shook his head.

John's mind held only one thought now, and it left him as strengthless to act as the touch of Death.

Will crept through the deepening twilight, moving from moss-hung rock to piece of wreckage as he and Doctor Smith worked their way toward the glowing gap in the hull of the *Jupiter Two*.

Smith put a hand on his arm, abruptly holding him back. "As soon as we enter," Smith murmured, gesturing, "I want you to blast anything that moves."

Will looked at him with a frown of surprise. "But shouldn't we find out—"

"Will," Smith said, unexpectedly putting an arm around his shoulders, "let me tell you about life. Around every corner, *monsters* wait. I know. You see, I *am* one. And we monsters..." Will felt his body try to shrink out of Smith's grasp; the Doctor's bottomless stare pinned him like a butterfly under glass "...we have no fear of devouring little boys. To survive, you must be fully prepared to kill."

Will shrugged off Smith's arm. "I can do it," he said, too loudly. He knew that Smith didn't believe the words, any more than he did.

"Listen to me, boy!" Smith said angrily. "I have crossed this world with you. I will risk my life—but I will *not* throw it away." He gestured at the alien world around them, the path of light spilling from the broken ship. "Who knows what dangers lie ahead? *You* cannot protect us, child. But I can. I will. So I ask you now, trust me . . ." He held out his hand. "Will. Give me that gun."

Will hesitated, wishing his mother was there, to tell him what to do; wishing his father would somehow miraculously appear, and make the decision meaningless.... Slowly, he pulled the pistol free. He thumbed the lock pad. "Enable gun for all users," he ordered.

"*Voiceprint confirmed,*" the gun said.

He handed the gun to Smith.

"*Finally—*" Smith's arm uncoiled like a striking snake. He caught Will around the neck, pinioning him, and pressed the gun barrel to Will's temple. Will cried out, shutting his eyes.

"A brief lesson in survival, on this world or any other," Smith hissed. "*Never trust anyone.*"

Smith let him go, shoved him forward. "Remember it into your old age . . ." he said, his voice poisoned with bitterness, "should you have one. Now move!"

Will started on numbly, fighting back tears.

John stood with his grown son, watching the hyperdrive basin; finally giving Will the kind of attention he had always wanted. In the glowing basin field dampeners were slowly compressing the amorphous energy bubble into a corridor of coherent imagery. An ever-expanding ring of plasma fire surrounded a blue-and-white-flecked sphere that even as he watched was becoming more and more clearly a vision of the Earth.

It was possible to travel through time *and* space, controlling your destination with pinpoint accuracy . . . without a hypergate. His son had proved it. The *Proteus* had done it. . . . He realized suddenly what he had not even had time to consider before: that whether they ever returned to Earth or not, their world was safe. *Humanity had reached the stars.*

Behind him West slipped into the shadows, moving toward the hyperdrive console, and the core material. If he could only keep Will's attention focused here, West would have a chance to act. It struck him painfully that he had never listened to Will before the way he was listening to him now. That he was fully appreciating the brilliance of his son's mind only now, as he performed an act of betrayal, and Will performed an experiment that could destroy the Earth after all.

"I can do what you never could," Will repeated, like a mantra. "I can save us all—"

"Never fear!" a sarcastic voice called out, across the room. "*Smith* is here."

John spun around, to see Smith come through the doorway behind the Robot, with Will . . . his son—his ten-year-old, frightened son—held at gunpoint. Smith pulled some kind of device from his pocket, and with one swift motion lodged it in the Robot's back. The Robot's arms flew up, then dropped to its sides. A *control bolt*.

"Will!" John cried, starting forward.

"Don't move, Professor Robinson," Smith raised the gun, his eyes cold, "or this rather peculiar family reunion will be tragically brief." He glanced aside. "I'll ask *you* to step away from that console, Major." He gestured West back.

West froze, staring at Smith, and Will. And then he crossed the room to join John without protest.

Smith stood behind the Robot, inputting orders on the control bolt's keypad. "I knew this would come in handy." He glanced up at them with a satisfied smile as the Robot abruptly powered up, raising its arms. "Let's try this dance again," he murmured, addressing it now as he finished reprogrammimg its CPU. "You are the puppet. I am the puppeteer. *Do* get it right this time . . . Robot, you will respond to my voice alone. Enable electric distrupters."

The Robot's extended claws began to glow as an energy charge built between them. Smith's smile widened. "Now that's a good gargantuan."

John glanced away from Smith, seeing the expression on his young son's face as Will gazed at the time machine, wide-eyed. "You did it," Will murmured. "Just like I imagined! Rerouted the hypercore. But the spatial delivery system . . . the modified power source! I never thought of those—"

Will's avatar looked back at him, with a bittersweet smile. "The future is never what it looks like when you're ten. . . ."

Smith crossed the room and put his gun to the adult Will's head. "Say good-bye to your past," he said. "Your future lies with me . . . I'm going home in your place."

The older Will turned to look at Smith; an amused expression spread over his face.

"An odd moment for merriment, don't you think?" Smith snapped. "What are you grinning at—?"

The older Will shrugged, and gestured at the room. "Look around you, Doctor," he said. "At this hostile world. Do you really think a boy could have survived, all alone?"

Smith's eyes narrowed; his frown turned puzzled.

Movement caught the corner of John's eye, and he saw —something— emerge like a fluid shadow from the deeper shadows cloaking the walls and corners.

A voice, alien and yet somehow horribly familiar, rasped, " 'Never fear, Smith is here . . .'" The shadow form moved into the light on clicking, inhuman feet. It wore a black, hooded robe pieced together from torn fieldsuits, tubing, and circuitry. The robe cloaked its seven-foot form, barely revealing a glimpse of a face covered with silvery techno-organic chitin. What had been hair and beard had transformed into spiny filaments that made John think of insect feelers, or insect limbs. The eyes glowed like polished metal in the reflected light. But somehow, undeniably, it was Doctor Zachary Smith.

"Hello, Doctor," the hybrid rasped, moving toward Smith, "how nice to see *me* again, after all these years." An arm flashed out of the cloak to slap the weapon from Smith's trembling grasp. The hybrid loomed over him, peering down at his face. Smith shrank back as though he were trying to fold in on himself and disappear.

"The spider's sting had some unexpected side effects..." The hybrid seized Smith and spun him around, revealing the tear in his shirt—the wound he had gotten as they fled the spider-aliens on the probe ship. John saw how the wound had festered, as the technovirus began to invade the cells of Smith's body.

So did Smith. He jerked loose from the hybrid's grasp, his face filled with terror.

"But my unique gifts gave me an advantage in this quarrelsome world." The hybrid reached out, caressing the older Will's cheek. For the first time, John saw his hand clearly . . . barely even a hand anymore.

"After the women were savaged," the hybrid said insinuatingly, "*I* became the father Will never had."

John's hands silently tightened into fists; beside him, West grimaced in disgust.

Abruptly the hybrid seized Smith by the arms, dragging him around the room like a doll in a grotesque waltz between past and present. "Three decades of agony taught me the error of my ways," he grated, bending

Smith backward until his spine threatened to snap. "But *you*, Doctor. Your crude ambition fills me with self-loathing!" He twisted Smith like a rag, twirled him back around. "You see, I have looked within me, and what I see is *you*—"

Suddenly he hoisted Smith up over his head; as his robe fell open John saw more spidery arms flailing at his sides. With a tremendous heave, the hybrid pitched Smith across the room, out through an opening in the wall, down onto the rocks below.

"I never liked me, anyway . . ." the hybrid muttered, straightening his robe. The words hung like a shroud over the stricken, silent room. He turned to the Robot. "Kill them all."

"No!" the grown Will said sharply. John looked up in sudden hope, but Will did not acknowledge any of them.

The hybrid folded his claw-hands like a praying mantis. "Be reasonable, son," he said placatingly. "Once your doorway in time is complete, this planet will come apart . . ." He raised a silver claw to his chitoned brow in an oddly theatrical gesture. "*Oh*, the sweet redemption of eternity! I am willing to perish here for your most noble mission, so that all our suffering will have never been . . ." He glanced at John. "But your selfish *father* will only try to stop you." He looked back at Will.

Will held the hybrid's gaze, impassive, unyielding.

The hybrid heaved a large, very human sigh. "Very well . . . Robot, take them inside the ship and keep them there. If they move, *then* kill them."

The Robot rolled forward and obeyed.

✳   ✳   ✳

Maureen looked up from the display screen of her remote as another tremor shook the ground around them, starting small dusty landslides everywhere. Birds or something like them screamed and took flight, reminding her suddenly of the urgency of their own situation. "We've got to get to the ship," she said to Judy. Judy nodded and looked around for Penny.

Penny wasn't there. Neither were the two Blawps.

"Penny—?" Maureen called, feeling her chest tighten.

Suddenly their Blawp appeared, skittering out into the open space to grab her hand, trying to pull her forward. Blawp's fist held a mass of colored ribbons—the ones that Penny always wore.

"Where is she, girl?" Maureen asked anxiously, as Blawp waved the ribbons in the air. Blawp raced off into the underbrush, still gesturing at them to follow.

Maureen looked at Judy; Judy shrugged. *What choice did they have—?* They went after her.

Within the *Jupiter Two*'s cannibalized engine room, the field dampeners were creating an ever clearer, more precise vision of the Earth within the conduit of temporal energy . . . narrowing its field of focus until John could see the familiar skyline of Houston. On this world, the ground tremors were increasing in frequency, shaking the unstable structure around them.

The Robot moved forward to herd them from the

room. John lifted his young son up onto his back, as the grown Will rode the control console up to the gantry. The hybrid clambered effortlessly up the scaffolding after him. John glimpsed inhuman arms and taloned feet again, flickering in and out of view beneath the tattered robe as Smith climbed higher.

West gasped suddenly, beside him. "Egg sac . . ." Don breathed, his face bloodless. John saw in his eyes the memory of Jeb Walker. The *Proteus* flashed into his own mind; he suddenly remembered the holograph of something its crew had brought up from the planet's surface.

"Will!" he shouted. "It's a trick! Smith's carrying an egg sac—if he's going to stay on this world and die, why is he about to *spawn*?"

Energy lanced between the Robot's claws as it approached. *"Proceed to the ship or be destroyed,"* it said.

Carrying his other son, the one he might still be able to save, he followed Don out of the room.

Will watched, thin-lipped, as the Robot herded his younger self out of the room, along with his father and Don West—both of them looking no older than the last time he had seen them, for the simple reason that they *were* no older . . . They had slipped through a gap in time opened by the very machine he had created. Time was no longer a river, but a vast sea, and riptides were eating away at this world's stability.

He had anticipated the time displacement that would tear this planet apart; but he had never dreamed it would mean that he'd see his father again, young and alive. Were his mother and sisters still alive out there too, somewhen; about to meet their deaths in a wholly different, but equally terrible way...?

As the platform reached its position on the upper gantry, the hybrid dropped into place beside him. For the first time in years, Smith's mutant body startled his eyes. He had forgotten how hideously changed from its original human form it was, until he'd seen the man again as he used to be.

Smith peered down into the temporal vortex, at the vision of Earth it was reeling in, closer and closer to the right place, the right moment. "It's almost *time* . . ." he said gleefully, and made a travesty of a chuckle. "I really am a word-*smith*." None of this seemed to phase him. But then, Smith had literally thrown away his younger self, with its reminder of his humanity, no matter how flawed. . . .

This shouldn't be a happy moment, Will thought. He might have spent nearly three decades alone, with no one but this monstrous caricature of a human for a companion, but he hadn't forgotten everything about how real people behaved. *His parents had taught him that, and his sisters, too . . .*

He looked up. "Tell me again, old monster, how *did* the girls die?"

Smith shook his head. "We've been over this before, son . . ."

"In all the years since, the spiders have never resurfaced," Will insisted, moving away from the control panel. "*Why?*"

Smith stared at him for a long moment. And then his

distorted lips widened in a smile. "Let's forget the past," he murmured.

Will turned back to the console, resetting the perimeters of the time portal. The dampeners pressed in on the conduit of plasma, narrowing its diameter, narrowing their view of the launch dome that now lay at its other end point.

"Careful, child," Smith admonished. "The plasma around the portal will rip a man to pieces. Haven't you made the doorway too small—?"

"Not for me," Will said coldly. He turned back to meet Smith's inhuman eyes. "But then, *I'm* not going, am I . . . ?" His voice hardened. "The spiders didn't kill the girls—it was *you*. I just never let myself see it. You kept me alive because you needed me. Because I could build this for you!" He gestured at the vortex.

"Poor, *poor* boy." Smith shrugged off his cloak; four grotesquely deformed hind limbs straightened out of their crouch. "Did you really think I would let you go home . . . ?" A second set of unnaturally elongated arms unfolded at his sides. "Let all that I have become vanish?" The obscene conduit of his neck snaked upward, rising from the carapace of his bloated thorax until he stood ten feet tall, revealing the hideous truth that he had hidden for so long. "*Look at me—!*" he commanded. "I am no mere man . . . I am a *god*."

He pulled open the egg sac at his waist, so that Will saw the swarming mass of countless spider-forms. "Within me lie the seeds of a master race. We will descend upon the helpless Earth. An entire planet to rule—" His arm darted out, grabbing Will by the front of his shirt, dragging him forward. Smith's mouth gaped wide over Will's throat, as he murmured, "An entire planet on which to feed . . ."

Chapter Twenty

Will sat beside his father, feeling another tremor shake their rapidly crumbling world. Festoons of conduit swayed, the piled rubbish and broken equipment creaked and rattled, until the storeroom in which they had been confined seemed to have a life of its own . . . like the Robot, standing guard at the door.

The Robot looked just the way he had imagined it would when he was finished putting its new body together: the two multipurpose work arms that carried the electric disruptor circuitry in the front; the single grappling arm, all he'd been able to find in the crates of replacement parts, in the rear. The tractor treads . . . That bubble diode really did make a great head—it even lit up when the Robot spoke. The only thing that didn't match his imagination was hearing it threaten to kill them.

"I'll run, draw its fire." Don West whispered to his father. "You may have time to get away with Will." He gestured into the jungle of broken equipment around them.

Will had listened while the men tried to figure out how to escape from this room. But with the Robot watching them, he knew anything they tried would be suicidal. Smith had made the Robot his prisoner, just like them. It was a slave to his orders, no matter what it really wanted to do. Unless . . .

He got up quietly and slipped away from his father's side. Step by step, he crossed the room toward the door.

"Halt or Robot will destroy!" The Robot turned where it stood, lightning crackling between its claws. Across the room his father and Don looked up in startled horror, as the Robot extended its arms toward him.

Will stood his ground, trying not to look afraid. "Robot, do you remember me?" he asked. "Do you remember what I taught you? About friendship?"

The Robot stopped in mid-motion, as if it were pondering the question. *"'Friendship means acting with your heart not your head,'"* it said at last.

Will nodded. "I need you to help us now, Robot. Because we're friends—"

"Logic error," the Robot said. *"'Friendship' does not compute."*

"Forget logic!" Will insisted. "Act with your *heart*."

"Robot has no heart. Robot is powered by a fusion pulse generator—"

"Every living thing has a heart," Will said softly. He thought of the grownup Will, and tears stung his eyes again. He blinked them back.

"My programming has been modified to remove all emotion." The Robot stood unyielding in front of the doorway. *"Any attempts to override command protocols may result in fusing my neural net."*

The planet rumbled and shivered beneath them again. *"Please*, Robot," Will begged, "if you don't let us go, we're all going to die! I'm asking you now, will you help us? Will you be my friend—?" *He had saved the Robot's life, once . . . did it still remember that? Could it?*

The Robot stood motionless for a moment longer. And then it reached around to its own back, toward the control bolt Smith had attached to its CPU. *"Robot attempting to deactivate control bolt*—commands overridden—*attempting to reroute—danger*—kill them, kill them . . ."* Its claws rose into attack position; energy began to arc between them. Will bit his lip, barely able to keep himself from running away as the charge built to maximum and it took aim at him—

At the last second, the Robot's arms jerked upward as it fired—the blast of energy tore a hole in the ceiling, and the Robot reached back triumphantly to rip loose the control bolt.

"You did it!" Will breathed.

"Robot will save . . . I *will save Will Robinson,"* the Robot said proudly. *"I will save my friend."*

Maureen and Judy chased the frantic Blawp through the undergrowth until Maureen thought she couldn't go any further . . . only to look up and discover that Blawp had led them right back to the portal where they had come through. Beyond its ring of fire, the *Jupiter Two* lay waiting.

They followed Blawp back through, just in time to see Penny emerge from behind the ship and sweep Blawp up in her arms.

"Penny?" Maureen cried in disbelief, and then in breathless exasperation, *"Penny?"*

Penny stood at the hatchway, beckoning them urgently to get on board, as if they were the ones who had inexplicably wandered away. They ran to the ship without question, and were safely in the elevator on the way up to the bridge before Maureen finally asked, "*Where* did you go—?"

"I had a promise to keep," Penny answered, with the self-contained logic of a fourteen-year-old.

Maureen sighed. Before she or Judy could ask more questions, another tremor rumbled through the ship, and shook every other thought out of all their minds.

John stood at the open hatchway with Don West, looking toward the engine room and the uncanny light radiating from it. The ground shook and rumbled under their feet.

"Without the core, we'll never have enough power to make orbit," Don said grimly.

John nodded. "See if you can find your way back to the *Jupiter*. I'll try to get the core material, and meet you there."

West frowned. "You're getting us confused," he said. He touched his chest. "*I'm* the one who stays behind. I'm the one without everything to lose."

John shook his head . . . and was suddenly sure, as he saw the expression on Don's face, that he had made the right decision. "No matter what happens, when the planet starts to blow, you take off."

West caught his arm. "John, the family needs their *father*—"

"The crew needs their *pilot*," John gestured at the twisted ruins of the ship they stood in. "I can't fly this ship as well as you can. You're their best chance to survive."

"But—" Don looked at him, his eyes suddenly lost.

"Listen to me, Don," John said quietly. "I know you never wanted this job. But I think you'll turn out to be a Grade A baby-sitter after all. So the camper's all yours, now...." He glanced down. "Take care of them."

Don stared at him for an endless moment. Then, finally, he murmured, "Good luck," and held out his hand.

John shook it; realized as he let it go just how empty his own hands were. "I could use a weapon," he said, scanning the area around them.

Will and the Robot reemerged from the ship behind him.

"Dad—" "*Professor—*" they said, in unison, "*—we have a plan.*"

The Robot extended an arm; a panel popped open on its surface. Will reached inside and pulled out the component he had soldered together only yesterday . . . and which had served the Robot well for thirty years. He had made it out of his gold medals from the science fair; he had felt proud—and vindicated—that he'd found a real use for them. He felt that way again, doubly so, as he handed the component to his father. The sharp-edged, jagged disk could have doubled as a ninja's throwing star.

His father looked down at it, up at him, without speaking. But Dad's sudden hug, and what his eyes said then, told Will everything he had always wanted to hear.

As Dad set off toward the engine room carrying the star, he looked every inch the hero Will had always known him to be.

Don West put out his hand. Will took it, and Don led him and the Robot away in the other direction.

Inside the engine room, the hybrid forced Will back against the platform's rail. "Time to die, son..." he whispered, and his mouth opened wider.

"I'm *not* your son!" Will brought his fists up with all the strength of his rage, smashing Smith in the face. Smith staggered back.

Will jerked free; turned back, as an alarm began to bleat on the control panel.

But Smith gave him no time, and the platform gave him no space. Smith seized him from behind, and heaved him over the railing into the darkness below.

"Good-bye . . ." Smith murmured, smiling. He moved toward the control panel without a backward glance.

Don led Will and the Robot away from the ship as quickly as possible; not just because time was running out, but because he didn't want Will to see or hear if something went wrong for his father. They picked their way down the rocky slope below the ruined ship, stumbling in the near darkness as the ground shook again and again. He hoped he remembered enough landmarks to get them back to the real *Jupiter*; hoped desperately that the portals were still where he'd seen them before.

They weren't. He hadn't gone three steps when he staggered to a halt, as a new portal's fiery saw blade slashed through the rock face and the ship's remains just ahead of them. A younger world, bright with sunlight, beckoned them from the other side. *But what time was it—?*

"Look!" Will shouted, pointing, but not at the portal.

Don turned, and saw Smith lying in a crumpled heap on the stones, where his mutant doppleganger had thrown him. Will ran to Smith and crouched down by him.

Don followed, more reluctantly. He kneeled beside Smith, checking his throat for a pulse. "Damn," he muttered. "He's still breathing." None of them would be caught in this nightmare, if Smith hadn't betrayed them. *Why couldn't life deal someone the hand he really deserved, just once—?* Don stood up and turned his back on Smith's unconscious body. He began walking toward the portal. *If anybody deserved aces and eights, it was Smith—*

"We can't just leave him here," Will protested.

Don looked back at him. "Sure we can." He gestured at Will to follow. Will's eyes filled with stunned confusion.

Before either of them could do more, the ground began to shake again, harder, the rumbling counterpointed by a howling blast of wind. Another portal tore open in the air high above their heads, dropping toward them like a tornado's funnel.

Don grabbed Will and ran, leaping down the slope to

level ground. The rift stopped falling, halfway down the crater wall. The crater's upper rim was gone, replaced by a flaming porthole; inside it, Don saw a sea of molten rock.

He spun around, barely keeping his feet, as another portal plowed toward them from his left, as the planet howled and rumbled. The ground shook constantly now, the sound of Armageddon deafened their ears. Terror rose in him until he thought he was going to be sick.

Don caught Will as the boy staggered, keeping him on his feet. *He didn't have time to panic.* If he lost it now, they were already dead—

"Those portals all lead to different times!" Will shouted.

The rumbling and shaking were getting worse, as if the solid rock under their feet would vanish next. Don looked from portal to portal hopelessly. "But which one leads us home—?"

Judy stared out through the viewport, barely able to tear her eyes from the scene outside as she helped her mother and Penny get the ship ready to lift off. Outside, portals opened and closed like flaming bubbles in a boiling soup of space/time. There was barely anything recognizable about the landscape anymore; she didn't even know where to look as she searched for Dad and Will, for Don, struggling back to the ship . . . *If she didn't even know where to look for them, how would they ever know which portal led home—?*

She glanced over her shoulder. "Penny," she called, "enable all the missiles."

Penny looked up from her work station, shaking her head. "But the warheads don't work—"

"Just do it!" Judy ordered, and began inputting data on her console. Working like a woman possessed, she saw the displays flash green as the missiles launched. "Fire in the hole!" She entered the final commands that would fix their trajectories. "So those sailors, they drew shapes in the sky . . ." She hit a switch. COMMAND ACCEPTED flashed on her screens.

Stepping back, she watched the missiles rise; their glowing trails showed her how they were dispersing in the upper air.

"Detonation," Penny reported. "Just the priming flares."

A score of tiny lights shone high up in the sky. "To help them find their way home," she murmured. *Please, please . . .*

And then she smiled, biting her lips as the lights fell into formation, painting a giant face of Daffy Duck across the deepening indigo of the evening sky.

"The doorways are collapsing!" Will called out, pointing.

Don looked up from where he kneeled, trying to wake up Smith, as the sunny portal cutting through the rock face suddenly winked shut. He looked at Will's expression, not sure whether to feel hopeful or more afraid: *Afraid.*

"Oh . . . The pain . . . the pain . . ." Smith moaned, coming to at last.

Don watched Smith sit up. *You don't know the half of it, you miserable . . .* He got to his feet before he did something he'd regret, just to shut Smith up. He was a soldier; Smith was the enemy. He would have left him behind without a second thought, if Will Robinson hadn't been there, to look at him that way. To make him remember that he was supposed to be one of the good guys . . .

"Don!" Will shouted.

Don turned around. Looking through the winter portal, he saw the glittering constellation that had suddenly appeared in its night sky. He laughed in incredulous relief.

It was Daffy Duck. *To help them find their way home . . .*

"*Danger, Will Robinson!*" the Robot said suddenly. "*Danger—*"

The shuddering ground gave way behind them; the earth split open like a gaping mouth. The Robot caught Will as he scrambled forward, pulling him onto its back as it rolled toward the waiting portal. Don saw the portal begin to flicker. He hauled Smith to his feet, dragged him along as he ran after them toward the dematerializing gate. *If he didn't go straight to heaven for this, it was sure to land him in hell . . .*

"Jump!" he shouted. The Robot hurtled forward through the shimmering doorway, carrying Will to safety. With a superhuman effort Don flung himself and Smith across the threshold just as the portal closed.

Maureen stared out the viewport, feeling every breath she took hurt her chest, as the ground around the

Jupiter crumbled like stale bread. Where were they . . . *where were they—?*

"Mom," Penny cried suddenly, "it's them!"

Maureen saw the handful of figures tumble through a closing portal and stagger across the broken ground toward the ship.

Penny ran to cycle the airlock. Maureen didn't remember taking another breath until they were all inside, and Will was in her arms, being hugged by her, and then by Penny, safe and sound.

With fleeting surprise she saw Judy hug Don West the same way, as if she never wanted to let him go again. . . . But she did, and as he stepped back, he gestured at his heart, flushed and grinning all at once. "I'm going to tattoo your name right here," he said.

Behind him stood . . . *the Robot? Smith? And . . . and . . .* "Where's John?" she demanded.

West glanced up at her, and his smile fell away. He looked toward the empty airlock. "The portal closed behind us . . . It was his only way back. I'm sorry." He shook his head.

The ship rocked violently; for a moment she thought it was her life that she felt, falling apart. The explosions that followed wrenched her back to reality.

"We've got to try and lift off," Don said, and she saw the pain in his eyes.

She took a deep breath. "We've already begun the preflight countdown."

He looked at her in disbelief.

She nodded at her children, and said evenly, "I'm going to save as many lives as I can, Major."

* * *

Tremors shook the engine room gantry, where the hybrid stood at the console on the control platform, watching the core material slowly descending. As the display read PORTAL INTEGRITY 95% he gazed down through the wormhole in space/time, hungrily contemplating his return home.

"My father always said evil finds its true form."

He turned, startled but not alarmed to find John Robinson standing on the platform behind him. He smiled as he saw the raw hatred in Robinson's eye's; savoring this moment almost as much as the one that would occur the moment after he arrived on Earth. *Yes, Robinson was right . . . so perfectly right.* That made his victory over space, and time, and himself, even sweeter. *He had found his true form, and it was good.* "You should have killed me when you had the chance," he said, his smile widening to expose his teeth.

"No," Robinson said steadily, "I couldn't kill the man. But I can kill the monster—" He lunged forward, slashing at the hybrid's face with a star-shaped blade.

The hybrid recoiled, and the blade missed its mark. He lashed out at Robinson; four arms and his own far superior reflexes sent the human reeling back across the platform. With one bound, the hybrid reached the place where Robinson had fallen. Robinson lay stunned, glaring up at him in helpless rage.

"Spare me the fury of the righteous." The hybrid craned his neck, opening his jaws. "I think there's time for a snack, before my trip . . ."

Chapter
Twenty-One

John gritted his teeth, holding his body motionless on the shuddering platform by sheer effort of will as the hybrid's head snaked down, its jaws targeting his throat—

At the last possible second he swung his arm; the knife-edged fighting star clutched in his fist laid open the hybrid's face. Silver-red blood poured down and out over techno-organic scales, as the hybrid jerked back in surprise.

And then he craned his head forward again, his expression full of mocking contempt. "Oh, the pain. The pain." He showed his teeth.

This time John grinned back. "You ain't seen nothing yet—" He feinted at the hybrid's face and then slashed low, ripping through the viscous membrane of the egg sac.

This time the hybrid gaped in disbelief, as his monstrous children poured from the sac, swarming over his body, rushing up his armored carapace toward the rivulet of silvery blood spilling down his cheek.

"Remember the probe ship?" John said, the words venomous with payback. "*These monsters eat their wounded.*"

The hybrid's expression changed; a hand flew to his bloody face. "No," he gasped. "Stop. *No!*" He staggered back, lost his balance as the platform shook, and fell over the side.

John scrambled up and ran forward.

The hybrid hurtled back over the rail, thudding onto the platform. The eight taloned limbs that had saved him when he fell darted and wove like striking snakes as he started toward John.

John rushed him, shoulder-slammed him backward. The hybrid staggered and pitched over the rail again.

A talon hooked in John's clothing as the hybrid fell, and dragged him off the platform.

John flung out his arms as he felt himself go over, grabbing wildly for a handhold. He caught the metal grillwork and wrenched his fall to a stop as the hybrid went on falling down and down . . . into the space/time conduit.

Time itself seemed to stop, as John watched the hybrid plummeting toward the vortex . . . as, in the endless span of a heartbeat, all his worst fears came true. He hung on and prayed, as he had never prayed before, that the laws of universal order had not utterly abandoned this star-crossed world . . . *not yet—*

The hybrid's falling body struck the burning plasma ring of the conduit's perimeter, instead of plunging on through to Earth.

John choked on a sob of relief.

He looked down then, hearing the hybrid's screams. His gaze was as pitiless and cold, his mind as empty, as the space between the stars. *Payback's a bitch*, his father had always said. At last he knew, in his gut as well as his mind, why Don West had needed to destroy the *Proteus*. . . .

"Take all the time you want to die," he muttered, as the inferno immolated the hybrid's monstrous form.

John pulled his battered body up the gantry's frame, centimeter by painful centimeter, searching the maze of metal struts for hand- and footholds. *He had to reach the console; stop the countdown and get the core material before—*

A sudden gleam of light caught his eye, far down the ramp that fed into the hyperdrive basin. He stopped climbing, and looked down. A human form lay below him, sprawled motionless on the ramp.

Will. It was his son—his grown son—lying on the slope. Will's unconscious body was kept from sliding into the basin below by nothing more than the silver chain caught in a seam of the metal grillwork. . . . *By the dogtags he still wore, after all these years.*

Even as John looked down, another spasm shook the engine room. Will's body slipped a millimeter as the chain began to separate.

Will . . . he had to save him—

He looked up again. The core cylinder had descended almost completely. There was no time left. *Another moment, and he would be too late to stop it—*

He couldn't do both.

Duty or love . . . It had always come down to that, in his life. He had always chosen the big picture: *the greater good, the burden of responsibility, the vain belief that he alone could save the world.* He had sacrificed so many of the things that he really wanted, missed so many of the moments that really mattered: *the real, profoundly human experiences that made life worth living, and human beings worth saving from themselves.*

And look where it had gotten him.

John swung out over the ramp, and let go.

He dropped down beside Will just as the weak link in the chain snapped; caught his son's wrist as Will began to slide. With the last of his strength, John dragged his son clear of the plasma hellfire that had claimed the hybrid.

His legs buckled; he sat down on the floor. Holding Will in his arms, he stroked his son's hair, mumuring, "Come on, son . . . wake up . . ."

Don watched the ground outside the *Jupiter Two* spew magma, convulsed by the death throes of this nameless world. *He was looking at Hell . . .*

He checked the com displays again; the ship was fully powered up—as fully as it was going to get—waiting for his signal. His fingers rapped nervously on the panel; he chewed his lip. *There was nothing recognizable left out there; no one caught in that could possibly still be alive. . . .*

Maureen dropped into John's vacant seat beside him and strapped in. "I kept hoping somehow he'd appear," she murmured, not looking at him. She stared out at another world brought to ruin by human fallibility.

At last she looked back again, as if she had finally

accepted the inevitable. "Let's go, Major," she said, her gaze direct and clear. She nodded at the com.

Don hit the button; heard/felt the thrusters firing, ready to give him all they had in his attempt to get this ship back into space where it belonged.

But it wouldn't be enough— He strangled the thought. John Robinson had sacrificed his life to give the family he loved into Don's safekeeping ... *because he was the best there was at what he did.*

He was going to save the family John loved . . . his family, now. *He'd seen things today he still couldn't believe; what was one more miracle, after all he'd seen?* "Piece of cake..." he murmured, under his breath. *Piece of cake—*

The *Jupiter* rocked on its struts as the land mass began to give way, falling out from under the ship on all sides.

"Good-bye, my love," Maureen said quietly.

He looked up, and saw the unshed tears gleaming in her eyes. He looked back at the com. "Engaging primary thrusters," he said. "Now!"

The vibration of the ship's drive engaging overwhelmed the quaking of the ground; the landing struts retracted on command. The *Jupiter Two* wrenched free of the crumbling crater wall, and began to rise.

"Come on, son. Wake up . . ." John cradled Will in his arms, protecting him as best he could from the tremors that shook the floor and set the spider's web of conduits and cables swaying.

At last his son's eyes flickered open. "Dad—?" Will said incredulously.

John smiled down at him. "I thought I'd lost you."

A wondering smile slowly formed on Will's lips. But abruptly his expression changed, and he said, *"The core—"* He struggled to his knees, in time for them both to see the core cylinder sink into the control panel. A blinding beam of amplified coherent light lanced from the hyperdrive initiator, striking the basin; siphoning every joule of power from the cylinder's radioactive core to stabilize the space/time conduit below them. The monitor on the platform flashed PORTAL COMPLETE.

Slowly Will turned back to John, shaking his head. "You could have taken the core and left, before it was too late . . . You saved *me*, instead . . ."

John looked at his son, at his son's disbelief, and felt something inside him break. It filled him with a pain more excruciating than any he had ever known, as it set him free . . . "There wasn't any choice," he whispered. "I couldn't let you fall. You're my boy."

Will opened his mouth, but before he could answer, the ceiling above them ripped open like a paper box, and they were gazing up at a portal. The sky beyond it was burning, a maelstrom of red and gold, as if the world beyond had been inundated by a massive storm of fire.

Don fought the controls as the *Jupiter Two* labored futilely to throw off the weight of eight miles of sky and escape the planet's surface.

Below them the land rolled and billowed, vomiting magma, torn by blinding explosions. Solid rock folded like plastic, giving violent birth to mountains that were as suddenly swallowed down again into the planet's core. The ship was shaking so badly he thought her damaged hull would rip apart at the seams, and still they were getting nowhere. "We're not getting any altitude!" he shouted hoarsely, although Maureen could see that clearly enough.

A tidal wave of stone heaved up directly in their path, towering over them, and he could only stare, his mind empty, as it began to break: as giant slabs of rock split off from its crest, falling toward them . . .

A shadow fell across him, across the com. He turned in his seat for a last look . . . saw Judy take Will and Penny into her arms, saw them all—each stricken face a mirror of death.

He looked back at Maureen, his eyes burning with grief. His last words were, *"I'm sorry—"*

The avalanche of stone smashed down on them like the fist of God. The *Jupiter Two* exploded, consumed in fire, as the dying planet claimed its revenge.

Will stood with his father on the control platform, watched with him, as beyond the blazing portal the *Jupiter Two* struggled to lift off, to do the impossible . . . only to be swatted from the sky, obliterated inside a fireball of light.

His father sagged against the platform rail; Will saw in his eyes the naked agony of a man who had lost everything—his family, his hope, his dreams. "I couldn't save them," his father whispered.

Will looked away, unable to bear the sight. His eyes fell on the time corridor, still held stable by the core material's focused energy beaming down on it from overhead. Now it showed him the inside of the launch dome, the day of the mission . . . himself, ten years old, walking toward the *Jupiter* in his cryo suit. Innocent, hopeful; with no knowledge of the future that lay in wait for him . . .

"So many years ago," he said softly, "and I can still feel it. Our sun. Our Earth. It's all I've thought about. Going home . . ." He turned to the control console and began inputting new instructions, altering the spacial and temporal paradigms. The images in the time gate blurred and fragmented, flickering past like pages in a windblown book.

"A long time ago," he went on, although his father wasn't listening, "you told a small boy that one day he'd understand how much his father loved him."

Now this world lay inside the conduit: He saw the *Jupiter Two* appear, the ship still powering up, still intact . . . moments before its destruction.

"All I could see was your need to go forward at any cost." He turned back to his father. "What you never showed me was your love. I lost that. Robbed by time . . ." He shook his head. "I could never see how much you cared . . . until now." He began to smile. *Now, he was going to take back everything that he had lost to time.*

Another portal tore through the room like a chain saw, taking away walls and more of the ceiling; a churning, terrifying darkness lay beyond it.

Will reached out for his father's hand, and drew him across the platform toward the waiting conduit.

Maureen dropped into John's vacant seat beside Don and strapped in. "I kept hoping somehow he'd appear," she murmured, not looking at him. She stared out at another world brought to ruin by human fallibility.

At last she looked back again, as if she had finally accepted the inevitable. "Let's go, Major," she said, her gaze direct and clear. She nodded at the com.

Don hit the button; heard/felt the thrusters firing, ready to give him all they had in his attempt to get this ship back into space where it belonged.

The *Jupiter* rocked on its struts as the land mass began to give way, falling out from under the ship on all sides.

"Good-bye, my love," Maureen said quietly.

Behind them, Penny gasped. "Look!" she cried.

Don looked up with Maureen as the ceiling began to swirl, becoming translucent, as if some alchemical change had transformed it into water.

And beyond its rippling surface stood John, gazing down at them, and beside him the grown man who was Will, smiling. Will laid a hand on his father's shoulder and looked deeply into his eyes. "Don't make me wait another lifetime to know how you feel," he said gently, his smile filled with longing.

Suddenly, he pushed John forward, sending him over the edge of the platform, into the conduit—

* * *

—and through it to the other end.

John plunged through the fluid ceiling, landing hard on the floor. Maureen was out of her seat and down on her knees beside him before Don could finish his astonished double take. She looked up through the portal again, and the joy in her face turned to sudden grief as she saw her son—her long-lost son—so near, and yet unreachable. Her other children gathered around her, staring up at him in silent wonder.

"Come with us!" John called, lifting his hand. But the conduit was already breaking up, like the world beyond it, disintegrating as they watched.

"I can't!" Will shook his head. "There was only enough power for one person, one trip, remember?"

"Will—?" Maureen called, getting to her feet, helping John to his.

"It's good to see you again, Mom," Will said, smiling down at her. "It's good to see you alive." His image blurred, as the limpid surface of the portal began to cloud over. "Don't forget me . . ."

"Never, baby boy. Never—" Maureen climbed the ledges of the console beside her, her face wet with tears as she strained to reach the hand that blurred downward toward hers. John's arms held her steady, lifting her until their fingers were almost touching . . .

The portal closed then, and he was gone. Forever.

Don bit his lip, looking away.

Penny stood wide-eyed and motionless, with Blawp clutched tightly in her arms; Will stood blinking beside her. Judy put her hand on Don's arm, as if she needed to prove they were both still flesh and blood. He put his arm around her.

John drew Maureen gently down from the ledge where she still stood, gazing up at the empty ceiling. "He sacrificed everything, for his family . . ."

She looked back at him through her tears. "He learned that from his father," she whispered, her voice breaking. She threw her arms around him, burying her face against his shoulder.

Will came to their side, stood staring up at them. "Dad?" he asked, almost hesitantly, as his mother moved away again, wiping her eyes. He reached up as his father looked down, and placed the dog tags in his hand. "I'm glad you came back," he said, still blinking too much.

John kneeled down beside Will, hugging him. "I just wanted you to know," he said, "I love you, son. I love you very much." Will hugged him back; the way it always should have been, was always meant to be.

Outside, the ground heaved and crumbled, making the ship lurch as its struts unbalanced. Don let go of Judy and headed back to the com. "The planet is breaking up around us—"

John stood up, as they all scattered to their stations. "Status?" he asked.

A tremendous crash outside the hull gave him his answer.

"We're doomed," Smith groaned, as Don passed by him.

Don stopped, wheeling around as he was suddenly

and unpleasantly reminded of the other man's continued existence—and the fact that the *Jupiter*'s fuel cylinders were still half empty.

"We're *doomed*—"

Don hauled off and punched him.

He looked down at Smith's body, sprawled unconscious on the floor. He shook out his hand. "Boy, that felt good." Rubbing his knuckles, he stepped over Smith and finished crossing to his post.

John's expression held a mixture of exasperation and profound empathy. "Get us airborne."

Don dropped into his chair, slammed in a CD, and with music jolting his brain like adrenaline, he engaged the primary thrusters.

The vibration of the ship's drive engaging replaced the shaking of the ground. The *Jupiter Two* wrenched free of the violently morphing crater wall and began to rise, as the crumbling surface below the ship imploded with a deafening roar.

Don fed the engines all the power the ship had left to give; the *Jupiter* bucked and shuddered, fighting with too much heart, and too little thrust, against the irresistable forces that dragged her down.

He fought to stabilize the ship's pitch and yaw, to maintain enough altitude to survive and still achieve the speed and momentum they needed. "I'm going to try to reach escape velocity—" He looked out the viewport as a shadow fell across the com.

"*No!*" John gasped. "We don't have the core material! The gravity well will drag us down—"

Don veered the *Jupiter* desperately off his planned trajectory, as the planet's convulsions heaved up an impossible seven-mile-high wall of rock directly ahead; he wondered what the *hell* kind of choice Robinson thought he had. "We might—"

"We won't make it!" John said, his face grim. "Trust me. *I know.*" His expression froze the protest in Don's throat. "We've got to go down."

"What?" Don gave an incredulous laugh.

"Through the planet, as it breaks up—"

"That's insane!" Don said angrily. The foundering ship fought his control like a deranged animal.

"I don't have time to argue!" John snapped. "I'm giving you a *direct order*, Major."

Robinson's face vanished down a hall of mirrors as Don met his eyes: *seeing every arrogant, unyielding, stupid bastard who'd ever had too much power over his life...*

And then, suddenly, his vision cleared. He saw John Robinson. "Yes sir. Commander." He smiled.

He turned back to the com, felt his heart stumble as he saw the impossible heights of the mountain wall cresting above them like a tidal wave, saw it beginning to fall...

Below them a chasm split open in the planet's contorting crust, so vast and wide that the world seemed to be swallowing itself, and he thought he could see clear down to its molten core.

He shut down the engines. For an agonizing moment the ship faltered, suspended between heaven and hell, while on every side of her the head-on collision of continental plates heaped up stratospheric mountain ranges like crumpled fenders. Skidding on an oil-slick surface of magma, the ponderous folds of stone poured toward the lips of the gaping split, closing in—

And then the *Jupiter Two* plunged straight down into the chasm, and the planet swallowed it like a fly. Behind them the jaws of stone crashed shut, as pieces of the world collided and were consumed.

The *Jupiter* and her crew fell down the rabbit hole like Alice, into a universe of blinding light and crushing pressure, bare seconds ahead of the planet's avalanching crust. *Caught between a rock and a hot place—*

Don controlled their freefall, his mind surreally clear now; as though it had passed so far beyond the limits of recognizable experience that he had either gone insane, or gone completely rational. *"Fly through the planet."* *That* was completely insane. And yet they were still alive . . .

For now. Their speed was increasing exponentially as gravity sucked the *Jupiter* down toward the planet's core. The temperature and pressure outside would keep on rising until one or the other killed them all.

Damn it, he thought, *didn't we just do this yesterday?*

They'd been using the sun's gravity well to boost their speed, when everything had gone wrong. He remembered the sun reeling them in: *heat, pressure . . . and speed.*

He leaned forward in his seat to stare at the displays. Of course. That was what John had meant. Only, John had expected him to get it, too. *John*, he thought, *if I live, I swear I'll go back to school for a Ph.D. in astrophysics. . . .*

A shadow fell across his face. He looked up and out, his eyes widening.

Above and ahead, an entire ocean poured down through a fissure in its shattered bed, falling toward the *Jupiter* like the primal flood.

Just call me Noah— He flipped the ship like a silver pancake and hit the thrusters, sent them arcing through a high-gee parabola, up and away from the plummeting slabs of continental plate, toward the city-sized waterfall.

"Everybody hold your noses," he yelled. *Where there was a way in, there had to be a way out.* The ship drove upward through the falling sea, slicing it like a laser beam as they flew upstream toward freedom.

The *Jupiter* burst through the ocean's surface—into another vacuole; Don vectored wildly as an iceberg hurtled past them and fell away behind like the collapsing seabed. He aimed the ship at a spinning funnel of rock, not caring what it was, because at the other end of the hole he could see the stars.

The ship shot upward through the corridor of stone. They were inside a crumbling volcanic cone, he realized—*and not a dead one.* Congealing lava and rocks the size of houses roared toward him: *One final obstacle, one last assault, before this world had to set them free . . .* and suddenly this was the best damn VR game he'd ever been inside of.

"Rock and roll—" He grinned, letting the adrenaline rush sweep him into the Zone, where a starship inside a volcano could do the impossible; where missiles of stone and bombs of molten lava could never touch him, or his ship, or the people he'd come to care about as much as his own life.

He made the *Jupiter* dance to his music, weaving and pirouetting through the firestorm of debris with never a false step or a millisecond's hesitation.

"*There*. A window—" John said, beside him, pointing.

He nodded. "I see it!" He banked the ship toward the opening. The light at the end of the tunnel was a starry sky.

The ship burst out of the volcano's mouth, into the night, rocketing upward through the dissipating remains of the atmosphere.

The nameless world fell away behind them, crumbling in on itself as they passed the limit of its lethal grasp, escaping into the silent depths of space.

Epilogue

Don rose from his seat, stretching knotted muscles as his body surrendered at last to relief. Finally able to stop looking at the stars, he turned to look back at his crew . . . at his family. John sat watching him from the copilot's chair, with pride and more than a little envy in his smile. Don grinned, pushing his hands into his pockets, as if it was No Big Deal.

Judy came up behind him as the others began to stir. "Nice work, flyboy," she said softly.

He turned around, and his grin widened. "So," he said, "I earn that kiss yet?"

She kissed him chastely on the cheek. "You earned that."

Geez, what does it take—? He shrugged, starting to turn away.

Judy's hand caught him, pulling him back around. "This one is on credit." She threw both arms around him, fusing her body against his as she kissed him, long and passionately, on the mouth. She let him go.

Don staggered back, speechless.

She smiled, raising her eyebrows. "'Cold fish,' huh?"

She glanced away as Penny's pet began to *blawp*

loudly and insistently; the distraction saved him from the embarrassment of any answer at all.

Maureen's amused glance left the two of them for Blawp. Her smile faded as she stroked Blawp gently. "Poor thing . . . She's all alone."

But even as she spoke Penny had begun to sidle out of her reach, taking the excited baby with her. Maureen said, "Penny, why are you looking at me like that? *Penny—?*"

Penny stopped again near the blast doors, safely out of reach. "I promised Judy I'd take care of her. . . ." she murmured, fighting a guilty grin. Her dark eyes fleetingly turned somber. "I couldn't leave her all alone." She turned, looking into the hallway, and called, "You can come out now."

An enormous creature stepped into the room, decamouflaging as it came. By the time its impossible form was clearly visible, Don realized it could only be an adult of Blawp's species. He shook his head. *And I thought orangutans were ugly . . .*

Penny let Blawp leap into its arms. The . . . *mother? father?—this is going to be an interesting story*—cradled the baby contentedly. Penny beamed while Will stood by the pair of aliens, looking up in fascination. Maureen sighed, as if she was already wondering what they were going to feed the thing.

John looked over at Don with a weary smile. "Now if we could only find our way to Alpha Prime . . ."

Will glanced back at his father, his face brightening. He nodded to the Robot.

"*If I may, Professor,*" the Robot said, from where it

stood watch over Smith's mercifully unconscious form. A holographic schematic of the galaxy suddenly hung in the air at the center of the bridge. Don recognized the familiar icon of the *Jupiter Two* among the stars. On the far side of the room there was another blinking point of light: Alpha Prime. *"Your son's star charts."*

"It's a map," Will said excitedly, coming to John's side.

John smiled and put an arm around him, nodding in fond appreciation. He looked up at the starmap again, so that only Don saw the fleeting shadow of sorrow in his eyes.

Alarms sounded suddenly, all around the bridge. Don turned back to the com, scanning the displays. Behind them in space, the nameless planet was bright red and pulsing. As he watched, it swelled like an angry blister and burst open, spewing a blast of pent-up energy and vaporized debris in a death cry that would echo through the reaches of space forever.

At her present speed, the *Jupiter* should be safe. By the time the shockwave reached them, its expanding shell of plasma should have dissipated enough to be harmless . . .

Don checked the displays one more time, just to be sure. Onscreen the core of the imploding world was shrinking again, growing smaller by the second, as if it was trying to suck itself completely out of existence.

He swore in disbelief as half the readings on the panel suddenly went off the scale. "The planet's gravity field is collapsing!"

"We'll be sucked in," Maureen said, looking toward her husband.

"There's no way to get clear in time." He shook his head.

"The hyperdrive?" Judy looked at her father, at Don.

Don nodded, pasting his smile back on as he took his place at the com and ascended his chair to the controls. John took his position, and removed the keys. He tossed one up to Don.

"Everybody hang on . . ." Maureen murmured, the words filled with more irony than dismay.

Penny rolled her eyes at her mother. "Here we go again."

"Cool!" Will said, grinning.

The nameless planet's core imploded, blinding the night, as the *Jupiter Two*'s warp engines engaged. For one brief moment the ship became a second sudden star against the darkness.

And then, like the world it left behind, it was lost in space.